Creative Souls

Poetry, Music, Art

Jackie Lowe

Acknowledgements

A big thank you to:

- The Creative Souls collective. Thank you for your talent, your words, your wisdom, your healing energy and your friendship.

- Tara Dominick for her incredible work to improve the lives of those in the Kakuma refugee camp. The world truly needs more people like Tara.

- Kuachi Gai, Den Min Yang, Mariamu, Mike Nyok and Pascal Placide - though we haven't met - your impactful words and captivating art have moved us. With the adversities you face every day, just know you are so deeply seen and heard. Your courage is a testament to the indomitable spirit within each of you. You are with us; we are with you.

- My dear friend Hugh Bearryman, whose inspiration sparked the vision for this book. Your unwavering friendship and creativity truly embody what it means to be a Creative Soul.

- My new friend Ben Street for helping me bring this together. Ben's own remarkable gifts have earned him a well-deserved place in the world of poetry.

- The Bedford in Balham, South West London—the birthplace of the Creative Souls endeavour, and a welcoming haven where creativity is free to flourish.

Thank you, beautiful souls. ♥

Much love and gratitude,

Jackie Xx

Contents

Foreword

There has been a tremendous revival of interest in poetry in the last couple of decades, especially in the English language, judging by the flourishing of literary journals devoted to such poetry right across the globe and across continents.

There is also another aspect to this revival. This is the mushrooming of venues and events offering opportunities for the spoken word, where established and budding poets can read their own poems to a live audience. While literary salons have been a feature of many large and thriving cities for centuries, and before that, of courtly life, these were often restricted to small groups of selected and invited people.

The phenomenon I am alluding to is much more democratic in nature, appealing to a wider range of both performers and listeners. Such open-mic sessions can be found in all sorts of venues. In London, for instance, the poetry scene that I know best, such venues often include cafes and pubs, public libraries and community centres, literary and neighbourhood festivals. Each venue or occasion has its own particular flavour or slant.

Yet, as often in a big city environment, there is a sense of fluidity, of people coming and going, with only fleeting connections with others. Having a kind of 'home base' where one can meet on a regular basis does wonders in helping to foster a sense of continuity. Equally important is having an anchor person who is always there to hold that space together, to meet and greet people as they arrive and make them all feel comfortable and at ease. This is the kind of home and support that I have found at Creative Souls in Balham, led by warm-hearted Jackie Lowe.

In addition to that sense of encouragement and support that many such venues provide to their poets, Jackie has taken a leap of faith by producing this anthology. The book showcases and provides tangible and material evidence of the work coming from the group. It will also enhance that sense of belonging to a community of fellow poets.

This poetry anthology also doubles up as a fundraiser for an arts project in Kenya. Part of the proceeds from sales of the book will go to the Kakuma Art Project, which brings art workshops and art materials to young refugees living in the Kakuma refugee camp in Kenya. This project was co-founded by British artist Tara Dominick and by Hubert Senga, a Congolese asylum seeker who leads Generation Aid, a youth-led charity helping young people in the Kakuma Camp. I am particularly thrilled to be supporting this venture as I carried out my first anthropological fieldwork in Kenya. I have also been closely associated with a refugee and migrant writers' group over the last two decades, namely Exiled

Writers Ink. I should also mention that I am a child of refugees, both my parents having independently fled Nazi Germany in the 1930s. My mother, Resi Clark, was herself an artist, with exhibitions in Rome, Berlin and Salzburg. Hence, the Kakuma Art project is one that deeply resonates with me.

David Clark

Introduction

After a difficult and challenging time in my life that led to a lengthy period of depression, I found solace in poetry. It was a cathartic and healing experience for me. Inspired by this, I decided to create a space where others could experience the same. I found a venue, and a year later, an amazing event that has continually evolved called 'Creative Souls.' We come together as a collective, a group of Creative Souls. Our words have become a source of healing for all of us, but also an inspiration for all of us - fuelling further creativity, with an array of beautiful art and with music in the mix too.

We have grown into a collaborative community that is welcoming and accepting - with no judgement and continual support - which really is greater than the sum of its parts, described by members as 'a spiritual warm hug' and 'alchemy… when we get together, something magical happens.'

What started as an experiment to see if poetry, spoken word, music and art would attract like-minded performers and audiences has now grown into regular sell-out events encouraging both first timers who have not shared their words before as well as more seasoned performers, who support and value each other's creativity - we laugh and we cry and we cheer and we have become friends - as Einstein said 'creativity is intelligence having fun.'

Who We Are Supporting

This poetry book collection supports the transformative work of artist Tara Dominick and the Kakuma Art Project, which brings therapeutic art workshops to refugee artists in Kakuma Refugee Camp, Kenya. Tara began this journey by painting Boat to raise funds for the first art materials, making it possible to bring paint into the camp and launch workshops that give voice to refugee stories, allowing them to be seen, heard, and valued. In partnership with Hubert Senga and Generation Aid, the project also funded the building of The Senga Gallery, a vibrant space that now supports art, poetry, dance, and community expression. A portion of book sales will help sustain and grow these powerful creative initiatives.

- Jackie Lowe

BOAT the painting that started it all – Artist Tara Dominick

Pascal Placide

Introduction

My name is Pascal Placide Nshangalume. I am 28 years old, born in Sud Kivu, Democratic Republic of Congo (DRC), and the firstborn in a family of five children. I arrived in Kakuma Refugee Camp in 2010 at a young age. There, I began my education and successfully completed both primary and secondary school, despite facing many hardships.

During my time in Kakuma, I experienced the devastating loss of three of my siblings. Though these tragedies were traumatising, they shaped my strength and resilience. After being abandoned by my uncle, who was my only guardian at the time, I became self-reliant. My difficult experiences inspired a deep commitment to advocate for fellow refugees. I could not bear to see others endure the pain I had faced without support.

In response to this calling, my two colleagues and I became the founders of Community Action for Peace and Solidarity, a grassroots initiative aimed at empowering and uplifting refugee communities. This remains one of my proudest accomplishments, a testament to my resilience and unwavering belief in creating a better future for others.

The Fire within Kakuma

Born where poor names poor,

I rose from the dust,

In Kakuma's heat, where survival is a must.

Not just a camp, but a forge of the strong—

A place where hardship sings resilience in song.

Education came not just through chalk and slate,

But through hunger, courage, and wrestling with fate.

Around me, young dreams often fade into haze,

Girls in early marriage, lost in unchosen ways.

Boys with empty pockets fill the silence with pain,

Dragged by addiction through shadows and rain.

Jobs are rare, hope even rarer still—

So we built CAPS with fire, vision, and will.

To teach, to lift, to pave a path wide,

Where youth gain skills, and walk again with pride.

For champions rise where chances bloom— From unskilled to skilled

Yes, I am raised in Kakuma's flame,

Where sweat carves dreams and courage earns a name.

About CAPS

Community Action for Peace and Solidarity is a Refugee youth-led organisation based in Kakuma refugee camp, supporting orphans through education & livelihood initiatives.

From Silence, We Rise

One family torn apart is too many.

Hopelessness settles as aid quietly fades, sirens replaced by the
hush of categories.

No one is born to exile, no child asks for chains.

No integration, no Shirika plan.

Our cries ricochet off walls that do not listen, and silence grows
where justice should speak.

We ration hope like dried maize.

Our children know hunger more than history; their dreams dissolve
beneath torn canvas skies.

They count us like census figures,

but forget we are stories, breath, and ache -

Not statistics stacked behind barbed wire.

Yet still we rise, uncertain, yet unshaken. We plant dignity in the
soil of broken systems, and craft rebellion from the verses of
silence.

We labour to bridge despair with dignity; one family torn apart is too many. We serve, we speak, and we stand for wholeness unyieldingly.

Post note - Refugees are wary of the Shirika Plan of Integration due to fears of losing legal protections, unclear rights, reduced aid, and challenges integrating without proper support or documentation.

SENGA

Created by **Tara Dominick**, Co-founder of the Kakuma Art Project, during a 10-hour sponsored Art-A-Thon, this painting helped raise the funds to build the first art gallery in Kakuma Refugee Camp. It symbolises the meeting of two worlds; Tara's own journey, represented by the refugee boat that launched the

Kakuma Art Project, and the deep connections she has forged within the camp.

The young girl is Abigail, the daughter of Tara's co-founder Hubert, reflecting Tara's affection for the community. The word *Senga*, written on the box, is Hubert's refugee name - used for safety - and also holds layered meaning: 'to ask' or 'to pray.' The boat floats on a sea of support, echoing the collaboration, solidarity, and hope that continue to drive the project.

Kakuma Artist Den Min Yang 'Pouring Bowls'

In this painting, Den remembers a happy time from his childhood, which contrasts with his experience of life in a Kakuma Refugee Camp. In camp, all bowls are made of plastic. But in his childhood, bowls were made of hardened mango skins and were brightly decorated. An especially exciting time for him was when his mother would mix milk and water in these lovely bowls and let him drink the sweet liquid through a bamboo straw.

Kakuma Artist Kuachi Gai

<u>*'Held'*</u>

The painting captures the stark contrast between the older generation and the younger women living in the camp.

A young girl is being held by the hands of an elder who is coercively holding her, pushing her to take traditional roles and early marriage, represented by the dark future on the right. In contrast, the bright, vibrant colours on the other side reflect the girl's dream of education and her desire to live life on her own terms.

Through this piece, the artist conveys the profound struggle many young women in the camp face, the tension between tradition and the hope for freedom and self-autonomy.

Kakuma Artist Mike Nyok

<u>*'Chained'*</u>

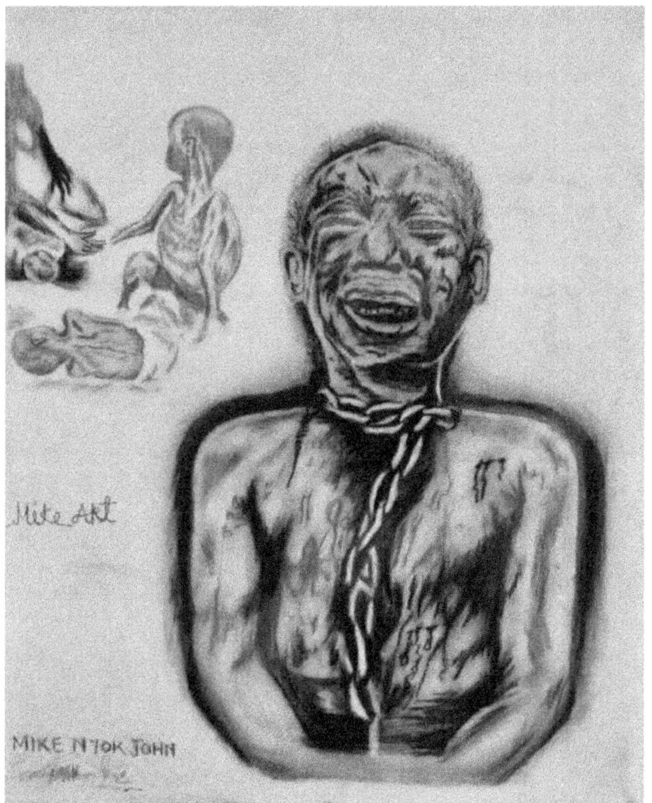

In this striking pencil drawing, the artist reflects on a tragic chapter from his life before arriving in Kakuma.

The man in the foreground was wrongfully imprisoned, accused of a crime he did not commit. As the family's sole provider, his absence left his wife in desperate poverty, unable to feed their children. The result was heartbreaking, her children became severely malnourished, their lives marked by suffering and uncertainty.

Through this piece, the artist captures not only his personal grief but also the devastating ripple effects of injustice on families and communities.

Kakuma Artist Mariamu 'Girl with Cheetah'

Mariamu has lived in the Kakuma refugee camp since she was a young child. In this evocative drawing, she explores her deep emotional bond with animals, particularly the dogs in the camp, companions she describes as the only beings she can truly trust.

For Mariamu, the dogs offer a sense of protection and loyalty that human relationships often cannot. The leopard in the image stands as a symbolic guardian, embodying the fierce and watchful presence she feels surrounding her.

This piece is both a personal narrative and a statement of survival, a testament to the power of connection, even across species, in a place where safety and trust are rare.

David Walsh

Introduction

Yorkshireman living in Glasgow whose de facto local is the Bedford Arms, Balham. It's a funny old 'Palatial' world.

The Palace at Applecross explains how this Yorkshireman living in Scotland happens to be included in this anthology.

Following the circumstances that led to the poem's emergence, I travelled regularly to South London for the football and chanced upon the Creative Souls poetry night. Consequently, as unlikely as it may seem, The Bedford Arms has become my more-or-less de facto 'local.'

Serendipity has surely played its part in my finding a place in these pages, and what a privilege it has been to stumble upon such a happening in Balham. It just goes to show: follow your own star and wonderful things may emerge from the mist. That certainly seems to be proving true for me. Good grief, Palace even won the FA Cup – glass duly raised!

As for Beyond the Machair: to chance upon a fine day on the west coast of Scotland, to brace for a swim in a body-shocking Atlantic followed by a picnic, a wee uisge beatha, and a sleep on the machair, is to have experienced some kind of dream-like paradise upon waking. The wildflower honey is optional, though much preferred!

The Palace at Applecross

I first saw that singular tri-colour years ago

Upright and centred on our very own chests

While here, cast askew, the claret, the white, the blue

Appeared as horizontal layers of pastel light

Suspended in late-summer evening's ethereal air

This was sunset at Applecross Bay

The iridescent flaming gold of our nearest, brightest star

Feigning to go down beyond the purple and grey peaks of the Isle
of Skye

And its related refraction, those aforementioned

Three bands of distant shadings

Evoking, transfixing from the south-to-east horizon

Spoke to me somehow of the classic strip of

Crystal Palace Football Club

I wore it as a boy, along with my brother.

It would prove to be the only complete kit

Our parents would provide for both of us

And we felt like kings when we first played in them

On Christmas day morning in the early nineteen-seventies…

First, the dribbling, those twists 'n' turns, crosses and saves

In our innocence, the goals were glorious!

But in this moment, holidaying on the Scottish coast

The high atmosphere haunting, like some sort of spectre

The trick in its light played on my grown troubled

For a somewhat experienced mind.

As the Earth spins on its axis

Creating each evening's repeat illusion

That darkness overcomes our fixed, broiling star

Here, conjured shades both awesome and familiar

Turned Highland splendour into anguished memory

And a passing: a profound reminder of him

Paralysing! Like a broken neck

Or, perhaps, a bereaved misting over glass

Our Palace above Applecross, then

Fading now…fading…fading

Each and every crystalised pane imaginable

Gently now…gently…disappearing

Then finally, if temporarily, masked behind the dusk.

Beyond the Machair

Sea spray

Is salting

The Machair

On chilling

Westerly winds

Still buffeting

The shores

Of the island

While its wild-flower meadows remain, untamed

Here in advance of the Mainland's rain shadow

An ambrosial manufacture is formed

From flora, through flight, to our honeyed jars

Courtesy of the worker bees of Colonsay

Jenny Malca Brown

Introduction

I was named "Jenny" in memory of the wife of Karl Marx. Politics has been generational in my family. I have children who are grown up and are wonderful humans. I am in the second stage of my life, that is I am over 70.

My life partner is a musician. I wrote lyrics to songs that led me into reading and writing poetry. I found the Balham poets by chance when I typed in "Poetry events in London Tonight." I loved it from the start, so I continued to travel more than 20 stops on the tube to be with the "Creative Souls."

I have poems published in various anthologies. Currently I attend open mic monthly at The Royal Society of Arts to contribute to the poems of the Cosmic Pumpkin. Poetry will always be with me and has been with me for many years. Recently I fell into short story writing which takes me back to many ideas I half developed but never finished.

I belong to a poetry group and take part in poetry in the park. In particular, I contribute poems to Hiroshima and Nagasaki Remembered and to Eco Events.

From Sounds to Words and Back Again

As music evokes memory,

So memories from music

Bring collective connections.

Whale song, through deep oceans,

Reach other Whales who are comforted.

Humans, spiders, worms and tigers feel the vibrations.

A choir stirs the sacred,

As listening awakens spirituality.

A river, bird song, sounds of rain fall,

Offerings from nature.

Sound through poems connects us to divinity,

Into stillness, silence into sound.

Born with sounds heard in the womb,

Born with the rhythmic sound of mother's heartbeat.

Laughter heard in every part of the Earth.

Sound, our last sense before passing over.

To listen, to hum, to chant or to sing,

Sounds have forever been existing.

January 2025

Belonging

They say the first relationship – the core one – is with yourself.

I was born into battle.

Young, when the army came with guns and bulldozers,

Terrified in my teens, running like mad from bombs and drones.

'Myself' traumatised, seeing bleeding bodies.

I shook!

I jumped at my own shadow. I cried. I tried to sleep.

I related to fear, loss, and anger.

Sad belonged to me.

Explosions flashed, fused sounds, deafening in flashbacks.

The panic suffocating,

Forever feeling the pain of others, hearing their screams.

They say the first relationship, the core one, is with yourself.

No, the core relationship is with death and dread when you belong
to war.

Never joined an army, never got conscripted, but your family,

living in peace before, has no rights anymore.

Ethnic cleansing leaves no belonging, no poems of children's
laughter.

Barney Low

A Poem

It's just a thought I had

That I thought was rather good

And thoughts they love to think some more

And be more understood

So letting thoughts and words collide.

On a page or iPhone note

Is just a way to let them live

And feed, and shout and bloat

So if the thought is clever or

Simply one that lends to rhyme

Is not a thing that one can know

When thought ahead of time

So this one seems

To be quite fun

But running low on steam

I hope my kettle

Fills back up

With wit and art and dream.

Aelita Kore

Introduction

I was born in Moscow in 1985, and I've been writing poetry for about 25 years. For quite a long period of time, I've been editing an online magazine about contemporary art and culture, collaborating with many different authors and artists and organising some events for our community. The first collection of my poetry, "From Sphere to Aeon," was published in 2023. A novel, "The Stylist," written in 2009, was published in 2024, and my epic poem "Journey to the Moons of Saturn" is going to be published this year, 2025.

I studied chemistry at Moscow State University and French literature at the University of Picardy Jules Verne, France, and astrology at Nightlight Astrology School, USA. After I had examined scientific knowledge, I moved to studies of poetic knowledge and then of esoteric knowledge, comparing these cognitive practices. I elaborated a visual art technique which allows me to develop a kind of universal symbolic language. My paper collages are part of a practice of alternative world views, illustrating the creative ability of our mind. We can enrich our perspective by using symbols from different cultures and being more flexible in a deeper comprehension of them. This could be a clue to a better understanding of each other in a more peaceful and healthier world.

"Who smiled during the meditation?" and "The day is over…" These poems were inspired by guided meditation in a Buddhist community in London and explore the complex themes of self and ego considered in Buddhist teaching and the Western psychoanalytic tradition in different ways. The first poem demonstrates the value of concentration and focusing on a positive inner spirit, and the second one plays with an intuitive introverted vision and some creative impulses. Poetry, being a meditative practice itself, can be a powerful tool for changing one's state of mind and healing.

32

Who Smiled During the Meditation?

Who smiled during the meditation?

And whose thoughts were bumping against the air?

It was nobody, but something was snarling there anyway.

Sensations of the room and people

Laid calmly on the sphere of water

But the sun has already gone under

Then what were those reflections on the water?

Was it me?

Oh, I wished it were myself

And this desire filled the room

Then vanished out of sight

And the dark fog covered the air

My thoughts are visible

They're dense and heavy

Like a swarm of coal or micro nails

for micro coffins

For all the micro-tombs of recollections

Of those who weren't sitting next to me

A newborn sunset took them away

The water was flaming with joy

And someone was behind it

My eyes are open; the walls are sky blue

White pillars hold geometry of vaulting

I am alive, mysterious and grateful!

The Day is Over…

The day is over

All monks are sleeping

And little boys and girls

Are having huge dreams

About the enormous space

They have been told of at school

But galaxies are still watching

With their black-holed eyes

What's going on on Earth

Magnificent archetypal beauty

And hidden gems

That they can never reach and swallow

Then astronauts see people

From their space cabins

Their dreams came true

They're playing with different planets

In their hands

And keeping the symbolic keys

In their pockets

Thin black lines of thoughts

Are crawling around the sun

And many people's egos are still walking

Along the streets

At night

Thinking of avatars and ancient magic

Erasing lines and other spots

From the sun's surface

Then, who can embrace our planet?

And all the human beings

All animals and every single conscience?

Wake up!

This task is not that easy

For a single loving inner world

And sleeping, archetypal beauty

Alex Barty-King

Introduction

Alex Barty-King is a musician and poet from South London. He writes, sings and performs songs with his independent rock band DAAY, who can be found at www.daay.co.uk. Alongside this, he performs around the UK at festivals with his storytelling group Tails Unexpected.

You & You

I write this down as a poem to you

To you and only you

It's been a wild ride and is certainly never over

I wait so long until I find you again

And miss you so much when you're gone

It's a whirlwind of exchange and delight

And upon meditation, knowledge and truth

A liberation from fault

A place to plummet and rise up in collaboration

I alone cannot do this; it is well known,

I need you to teach me, but it is I alone who must learn

I am tangled in business that I cannot shake,

Nor would want to for my own sake

Just please remember when we meet again,

To welcome me kindly, my dear old friend

We're buried so deep so we don't forget,

Long since forgotten but always found again

This is why it's joy and why it's delight;

To find a friend in the middle of the night

I'll never forget, and that's why I remember

I receive the truth because I am the sender

I'll never forget, and that's why I remember,

I receive the truth because I am the sender

Angel

Her hair, the hair of Angels

Locked inside a dream.

She lets me stroke her skull and hold her

Every want and need

And from my stare, her eyes nestle

In the curved frame of my nose

Now her locks are more inviting,

Her skin more soft and clean.

So, I hold her head, and I know she loves

The hand she cannot see.

And in her eyes, like stones of beauty,

I rest my worry; my heart is sewn.

Arjuna Kavian (sample from the 'Blackbird Anthology')

My City in the Rain

Sometimes the storms give us everything we need
And I can hear the rain trying to breathe
life into my dead city.
And I can hear the gutters flooding,
and the cardboard cut-out homes of the poor softening,
and all the horrible people
leading horrible lives
just stop being horrible,
if only for a moment,
if only to listen to the rain.

To listen to something deeper than themselves,
to remember what it felt like to have a god,
to have a moment where you are utterly mesmerised
not by beauty or by power or money or sex.

But by the sound of the earth
telling you,
you are something more than your pain.
And all that is worth having in this world
can be heard in tonight's rain.

My Mother, The Genius Refugee

In my mother's kitchen

I learnt how to draw

The European borders of African nations

And how to memorise more than just

My times tables.

I saw a bruised woman

With a lifetime of potential.

I saw the encaged math teacher,

The shy genius,

Who fed us with her hands.

And I saw potential stuffed

In a hollow doll.

And despite

All the cold air

And frost between us,

Today, when I put on my stiff tie

Onto my stiff body

And clean my motorbike

In the morning cold,

And ride straight into my classroom

I try and be the teacher

The world never let my mother be.

Ben Street

Introduction

Ben is a recent graduate in English and Creative Writing from The University of Exeter. His passion for poetry has grown throughout his time at university, leading to him creating a TikTok page that has grown to over fifty thousand followers.

Cataclysmic

It's an interesting word

Isn't it? But does it need more?

You don't know which route it's going

To take you down just on its own.

For example, I might reference

A cataclysmic reaction. What comes to mind?

Is it the cataclysmic reaction

Of the IED that flew into your bedroom window?

Or your wife discovering you didn't empty

The dishwasher before she'd asked you.

Which cataclysmic reaction is bigger there

I'll leave up to you.

Still, this poem hasn't left the cataclysmic

Mark of my ex-girlfriend's final message to me.

But then again, the thump in the chest

Was pretty cataclysmic when I saw her

Just three weeks later – the punch she threw

Wasn't bad either.

Violence is never the answer.

Unless you type cataclysmic definition

Into Google. Then you'll find it is the answer.

It's also the answer if you find yourself face-to-face

With an Arsenal fan, for their

Cataclysmically horrendous decision

Of which football team to support.

So cataclysmic can touch anyone,

Even you reading this… unless

You don't know what it means…

Though, if you don't know by now,

Then you're a cataclysmic imbecile.

Matrix Mayhem

Every day, I find myself stuck in the Matrix.

This neurosis turns me into Neo; each move I make

Is a bunch of red pills or blue pills. Call me Keanu

With a blue pill; I'm neurologically flawed Neo

With a red pill; I'm John Wick when they took his dog.

Are you ready to see how deep my rabbit hole goes?

It starts with easy dilemmas like a coffee and an epic by Dante,

or a Guinness and dark chocolate? The answer is clear;

then, once that G's been split, my gourmand tendencies set in.

Do I keep it British with a pint and a scotch egg, or a

Scotch and some punk's head? See, that's the red pill

For sure, and some days, it just tastes so much nicer

than blue.

So, a therapist told me to find a balance.

I took that as some red and some blue, but

Red and blue together though usually ends

In me banned from all bars except the iron ones,

Oh, and another phone call to you.

Bettina Schroeder

Introduction

Bettina Schroeder is a London-based multimedia artist. Her works include painting, poetry, sound art, and video.

Bettina escaped with her family from the former East Germany, grew up in the VW car town and later studied in Berlin. She moved to the UK in 1982, where she works from her London studio. She has exhibited internationally and performs sound art with spoken word throughout Europe.

Her book of poetry, 'Flirting on an Escalator,' was published in November 2024 by London Poetry Books:
https://www.londonpoetrybooks.com/shop/

Recent performances of poetry/sound art with spoken word and exhibitions include:

London Improvisers Orchestra - Performances with The Noisy Women group – Exhibitions/poetry Frauenmuseum Bonn, Germany - Cafe Oto events - Poetry & Exhibition events at: 'Crunch,' 'Skibabble,' 'Paper Tiger Poetry' and others - 'MOPOMOSO' events, Vortex Jazz Club' - üF-Beat Fringe Music Club night at Crouch End Literary Festival - Otolith group exhibition & music, Greengrassi Gallery, London - 'BOA-TING' with Steve Beresford - Neil Marsh's Vanishing Point at AMP Studios – Exhibition/poetry, Anna Göldi Museum, Switzerland – Exhibitions w. poetry performances with The Tunnel Artists group, Hundred Years Gallery, London – Oooh International Improvisation Festivals- Album releases (sound w. spoken word) with airplay at

BBC3, BBC Introducing, WFMU New York, 2BOB Radio, Australia, Resonance Radio, London.

More info: https://www.bettinaschroeder.net/

Album VERSUS by Jude Cowan Montague & Bettina Schroeder, VIDEO: https://www.youtube.com/watch?v=l4ZVIdgNalU&t=79s

The Passport

I am not searching for credibility
Up there at the embassy
But they hold the key
To my destiny
My ID
Don't you see?
They need to know
It's me
Check that passport
At the airport
I must be base-able
Chase-able
Traceable
Not erasable
Exist in paper form
That is the norm
Biometric, electromagnetic
Start with ink pad
Messy and black
Then print fingers
Ghastly colour lingers
And a photo, of course,
For better and worse
Not aesthetically pleasing
Accuracy not increasing
An image without smile
Makes me look vile
Like an inmate on leave
Unrecognisably brief
No reflection

Of my delicate complexion
Skin tone aside
I am obliged
To get legal
The process is lethal
Tick the box for my race
Gender and case
Be registrate
And in my case
For the authorities
National duality
Becomes a calamity
So, I fill in the form
Place where I'm born
Make the application
Explain my situation
State my Nation
Update information
In ten-year rotation
After which duration
Witness to trips abroad
ID gets tired and bored
Needs a fresh cover
Security feature buffer
Be digital and tougher
For the microchip lover
But you soon discover
Questions unimaginable
Forms impenetrable
And it's never enough
They want ever more stuff

Copies and originals
Of related individuals
Complementary data
Full curriculum vita
For the minimum
Of one Millennium
For every spouse
For every house
With details to forage
Did you live in Norwich
Did you ever eat porridge
Were your grandparents married
When your grandmother carried
Your beloved pater
In a perambulator
Did they have measles
Did they keep weasels
As pets
Where they a communist threat
What colour was your hair
When you came over here
And had an affair
Did you have permission
To hold a position
In public vision
And - this is vital
Do you hold a title
How shall we asses you
How to address you
Mrs, Miss, Ms or Mr
Lady, Doctor, Professor or Sister

Have you left school under a cloud
Did your family eat Sauerkraut
Do you prefer an Umlaut
Or French accent
No, the rules cannot bend
Go to the end
Of the document
Where you are meant
To sign with the date that you sent
The before mentioned document
If you want to extend
Or amend your passport
Don't forget to determine
That your parents are German
Not from Russia or Peru
Let us know
How they got through
In 1933, when Hitler had his coup
Did you read 'Mein Kampf'
"Das Kapital" or Emanuel Kant
Even the colour of your underpant
Could be relevant
Can you ascertain
That your mother wasn't flirtin'
Behind the Iron Curtain
That B really IS your physiological brother
And not Paul Merton
Have you been seen in 2019
With the singer from Queen
Where you keen
To study this form

Adhere to the norm
Things are getting Kafkaesque
But even if you're not from Bucharest
You must not rest
Lest you become transitional
Undesired or criminal
End up in a terminal
Hurry up, hurry up
There is urgency
In the workings of bureaucracy
Hurry to the embassy
Grit your teeth and pay your fee
Only in required currency

But one last question from ME:
Will my new ID
Be with me
Before I die in agony
Will the f…ing thing be mine
Before I am running out of time?
The reply comes instantly:
As soon as we trace
Your data, your face,
Fully consider your case
Your passport SHOULD arrive
While you are still alive.

DISPLACEMENT

Description

Applying for the renewal of my German passport while being of dual nationality brings additional difficulties, but I had not anticipated the many levels of byzantine bureaucracy involved in confirming my German ID. Surprisingly, the renewal of my British passport would have been relatively simple by comparison!

Ladies and Gentlemen

Twenty-seven degrees Celsius in the sun

Summer festival time

The fun has just begun

There's plenty of water, plenty of beer

Other substances sublime

And by the trees, green cubicles in a line

Cause the queue for the Ladies is always longer

But the smell in the Gents is much stronger

I came all the way from Telford

Hungry for music, tickets in my hand

It was quite an effort

Check-in, wristband

Get a snack, buy another drink?

Green cubicles are on the brink.

Cause the queue for the Ladies is always longer

But the smell in the Gents is much stronger

Let's check out the boxes later.

Main stage is starting up

One more lager in plastic

The band is rocking steady

And everybody is fantastic,

Except I need to get ready

Cos the queue for the Ladies is always longer

But the smell in the Gents is much stronger

The facilities are crowded,

People anxious with retention

The cubicle fills me with insanity

In stumbling out, I mention

The paper's run out

And the row outside snakes to infinity

Cause the queue for the Ladies is always longer

But the smell in the Gents is much stronger
<u>Description</u>

The poem was a direct response to being at summer festivals.
Observing the pattern of festival organisers as they unloaded yet
again too few portable toilets from a lorry, I felt compelled to share
my experience.

Chloe Lauren Smith

Introduction

Chloe is a London-based poet and community builder who has worked with people from all walks of life. A seasoned traveller with a stint of living in Zimbabwe, she has always written. She believes that creativity heals people and helps them to make sense of their own thoughts and feelings. She definitely benefits from the therapeutic edge of writing for herself. She never set out to share her work, just to create for her own sake. Yet, a few years of the open mic circuit, and the publication of her first poetry book 'Small Pockets of Mischief' as well as a regular Cabaret Open Mic in Croydon 'Skibabble' that she runs, here we are, welcome.

Have a Day

Today, have a day.

Not a great day, or an awesome day, nor a day to note.

Have a day anyway and it's OK!

Gliding through on autopilot, clinging to hope.

Get up anyway, with sleep-deprived eyes that sting, while your body sings to a lesser tune.

You… WILL… BLOOM… AGAIN.

Brush your teeth, wash your body and feed yourself like a friend, with nourishing things, small beginnings.

Doing the basic things, in the valley, you walking in… is climbing Everest.

Give yourself a rest. You are doing the best you can, navigating this land without a map.

The unknown but you are hardwired for home.

These get-through days are part of the passage and way to a better space and place. Wipe the shame from your face.

Better days will come, but if you can embrace this one.

In all its messy imperfections, this gift, the present you.

Then you are making things new and the hurting shards you learn
to hold with love, turn to gold.

Making you whole and beautiful.

So, have a day in the most mundane of ways.

And in time, you will see the beauty of the valley.

Returning back to the world and back to yourself.

Grateful that you looked to the skies and whispered, 'Help.'

Bird Song

I hear them awaken the dawn, dancing on the edges of endings and beginnings.

I think I understand why they sing.

So long and dark and still has been this wintering.

I understand why the birds sing.

Where have been the bookends of death and decay; they circle back and relay where life has always been.

I know why the birds sing.

Gathering up the first rays of spring

I can hear the birds sing.

They sing in the darkest moments of the night, before they feel the warmth of first light.

For they know the sun will never fail, they let their little lungs prevail.

With tweets and chips of frost-filled hope, a canvas for their grateful notes.

Coaching fourth the buds of trees and waking up the surly bees.

Christopher N. Chilton

Introduction

Born in Tooting, Christopher grew up in a B&B welcoming guests from all over the world. He was lucky to be told many stories about cultures both past and present which inspired his love for words, poetry and all things universal. His poems are rooted in his love for the spiritual mysteries of life and the interplay between the individual and collective underpinned by nature and the great unknown.

I The Fool

I foolishly go
Where I have foolishly gone before
To pursue foolish things and understand my foolishness that little
bit more, and to find answers as to why I've been so foolhardy
more than once before

I foolishly go
Where I have foolishly gone before
To foolishly know what I don't need to know
To foolishly admit what I needn't have done
To foolishly accept my choices and chaos as one

I foolishly go
Where I have foolishly gone before
Because how else can I know how foolish I truly am
And know how foolishly far I can go?
You see, I have this inkling.
There is always more to know.

I foolishly go
Where I have foolishly gone before
Because part of me loves being a hedonist, but heart says, please
no more.
My brain likes to remind me, I am the fool, whilst my body yearns
for another dip in that hedonistic pool.

I foolishly go
Where I have foolishly gone before
To learn what it means to begin, to end, to live, to die

I strive, I seek, I explore, I wonder why
Always in a circle on a wheel spiralling through space and time.
A simple fool, discovering this place, this face, this mask I call
mine.

Description

The Fool is the entry point into the Tarot deck and the Wheel of
the Year. It is a powerful and interesting card represented by the
No. 0. We are all fools at one point or another, and one way or
another.

The Flower of Life

A man was digging for treasure when he came upon a flower.

He looked upon its curves; he admired its elegant power.

It was pretty and simple, with circles for a face,

harmonious in energy, and easy to retrace.

The man found it drawn on many walls, by many hands at many
times.

Centring where many humans explored their many minds.

Hour upon hour he studied the form and flow,

the more he discovered the more he came to know.

From mathematics to geometry to the stars and beyond,

the man had discovered a symbol, a universal bond.

During my time in Essaouira, Morocco, I immersed myself in the art, music and stories of the region, uncovering many insights and connections.

Kliché Kingston

Introduction

Kliché, originally from Birkenhead, has worked as a cleaner, actor, lecturer, head teacher, and bluecoat at Pontins. Across six decades, Kliché has continually written and performed poetry.

Kids

Posh people get all the breaks.

Poor people just get break-ins.

Posh people kids get fancy Dan internships,

At daddies and mummies et al fancy Dan places.

Poor people kids get to be dogs-bodies wherever,

Never where they want.

Posh people kids get time-out

To practise the organ at church,

Time-out of school for music, dance,

Chess, sports, be the big I Am.

Poor people kids, bottom of the heap kids,

Just get Time.

For weeing in the street, stealing sweets,

Finishing off rats.

Posh people kids just get nice police chats.

What a start they all get to their fulfilling careers.

The starting lines, so differently drawn,

According to where they are all born.

But all of life's unfair.
So, suck it up kids.

Redraw the finishing line.

Don't let heritage bind you,

Don't let systems define you.

Just train, run, learn, try harder,

To put all you want

In your hard won larder.

Biscuit Corner

She sends me up the shop,

Half way down the road.

For Five Park Drive and a can of beans.

Not bought, on the slate,

It's a clock-work date, Wednesday.

Child-benefit, runs out at such a rate.

But today it's "No"

Just one for now and one for Ron.

With dignity all gone,

I say "yes please,"

With eyes cast down

At the broken biscuit tin.

"Hey girl!" the shop-keeper says,

With a funny smile on her face,

"Hold yer dress up, and grab a pile.

Hold em in yer dress,

And give us a little smile, eh?"

I gratefully obey,

Off I run...

I'll eat today.

Description

Inspiration for the poems:
Both poems are informed by childhood poverty and
witnessing social injustice.

Leonor Tinajero

Introduction

Leonor is a London-based multifaceted artist with Spanish heritage.

During the last six years, she has explored her creativity to connect with beauty and her emotions and those of others.

Her creations, both word and art pieces, are raw, spontaneous, visually breathtaking, universal and eco-conscious: Macramé, latch-hook, poetry, acting, live performances and more.

She has released an EP with Electronic Producer Gashnois titled Light and Dark, in which her poems take a more intense turn with the depth of Gashnois' pieces.

Her work has been curated and performed in some of the most prestigious spoken word events in London, such as Collective Souls, Anthroplay Theatre Anthrotalks (Hope and Desire), Dash the Henge Store, Lost Souls Poetry and her creations are displayed all around the world, from Madrid, London, to the US.

She works with businesses to make emotions and creativity part of the decision-making process with the aim of creating a more conscious and connected world.

Here is a link to an EP with my poetry and Gashnois's that has just been released:

https://open.spotify.com/album/1WvUimVYJv4XHuw7ap69IO?si=594SEsu4SR-PxX7ebDKSEQ

And here is the Grieving Your Love link:

https://linktr.ee/grievingyourlove

Finally, here's the link for Leonor's macramé work

www.leonormacramaker.com

and her work with businesses

www.sparkyourchange.co.uk

Grieving Your Love

Grief shows as anger

Today

A physical intensity

I don't want to stop.

I jump on you

And RIP your chest apart.

There it is… your heart,

Beating for someone else

Or just beating.

I focus my anger on it,

I grab it,

Pull it out

Of

Your

Body.

My hands covered in your blood,

And your heart is still beating.

Do you feel the grief now?

I want you to hurt.

Your

Heart

To

Hurt.

I tighten my grip.

My nails and fingers

Close,

Closer,

Tight,

Tighter.

Do you feel my grief now?

I tighten it even more

And I scream.

Your body is still motionless.

You are still looking at me.

With that condescending smile

My screams suddenly

Freeze you.

Can you see me now?

Can you finally feel my pain?

My grief?

The emptiness you left?

The future I envisioned

For us.

But I haven't finished

With your heart.

I look at you now.

Your eyes stoned,

Looking at mine.

But you still don't move.

I challenge you.

Show me your pain

The way you showed me

Your passion.

But no, you keep it all

In.

Tamed.

A frozen scream

A tighter grip

Your heart trembles.

And with all my strength,

I throw it

As far as I can.

We stare at each other,

And with fear we look

It is still beating.

Barely.

It landed

So close to where you left mine.

But still apart.

Do you understand my grief?

You took my heart.

And left it someplace

When satiated,

You feared I could,

Maybe

Just maybe

Reach your soul.

Your

Heart

Is

Screaming

Now

Loud

In

Grief

And I look at it

Look at you

And I smile.

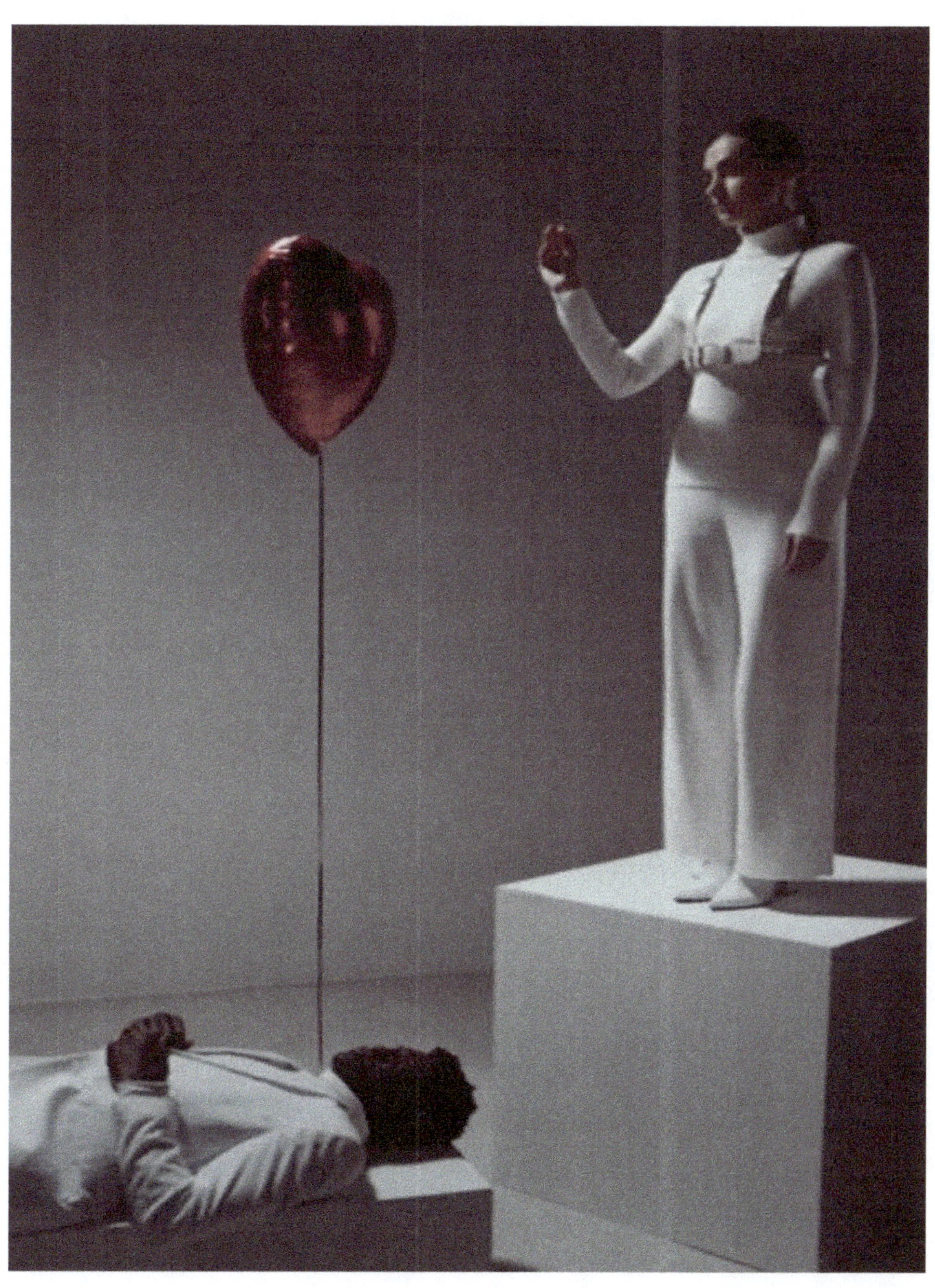

I am the Goddess

I am the Goddess of **Deftness** coming Alive

Tantalising life with the waves of my body

Mellifluously guiding all to a place from which

You can't come back.

I am the Goddess of **Ecstasy**, eccentric, forbidden, playful.

Embracing all simple things and making them grandiosely joyous

Making you dwell in your forever curiosity

Of what forever Joy can be.

I am the Goddess of **Poetry,** bringing us back to life.

Turning daily words into meaning-encrusted resplendent gems.

Preserving the magic of what your words mean to me.

I am the Goddess of **Beauty**, balanced, peaceful, alluring.

Turning your broken life into a magnificent piece of art.

Immortally crafted. Glamorous. Calm.

Stopping the whole world so it can witness us.

I am the Goddess of **Sensuality,** clenching your thirst

For more.

Coaxing the magic within You

Embracing the turbulence and power of all your emotions.

I am the Goddess of **Love**, welcoming you, your wholeness.

Even the one that chooses to leave.

Emanating romance. Slow patience. Loyalty.

Caressing your soul with the clarity and safety of a Mother.

I am the Goddess of **War**,

Water when challenged.

Earth when shaken.

Fire when loved.

Air when abandoned.

But always whole and strong.

Knowing what needs to be conquered.

I am the Goddess of **Life**, turning on your light.

Go and share your life-force with the world.

Travelling through times and universes

Where you live again. You are unstoppable.

I am the Goddess of **Lust**.

Can you hear the hum of my pussy calling you back?

I can use the gentle force of my hand

Or the violence of my soul.

I am the Goddess of **Wrath.**

Impervious to bullshit.

Immune to nonsense.

My anger can teach you how to master pain and fear.

Come to me!

I am the Sorceress of your will. Your desires.

Weaving spells with everyday's magic of language.

Challenging your beliefs by bending your thoughts

With prohibited paradigms.

My words will alter the course of events.

I summon.

I vanish.

I transmute.

I command.

Revere.

Now.

Are you strong enough to kneel?
Description

These two poems by Leonor Tinajero are the first and last poems
performed at Creative Souls Event at The Bedford. Leonor's
poetry started as an emotional release to express her frustration and
anger because of the end of a relationship. **Grieving Your Love**

allowed her inner violence, anger and frustration to be alchemised and challenged in a way that she never thought would be shared and understood by so many. Especially women who are not normally allowed to express those emotions.

I am the Goddess who honours all her inner parts and those of so many women who struggle to see their inner selves because of societal expectations and standards. I am the Goddess is an Ode to inner feminine power, empowered by both women and men.

David Clark

Introduction

I discovered Crete in 2003. I had just completed my doctoral dissertation on tourism and heritage management, and I was looking for a new project to do. A newly renovated synagogue in Crete was looking for a volunteer for the summer to show visitors around the synagogue. I applied and embarked on a new adventure. I have been returning to Chania virtually every year since, setting up my own research project on how English-speaking expatriates are adjusting to life in Crete.

My second poem is about another discovery I made a few years later, about what singing and writing poetry have meant to me.

***

David Clark's poems are published in Contemporary Writers of Poland (2015), Exiled Ink (2018), The Litterateur (2021), Change is the Only Constant (2021), Mediterranean Poetry (2022), Southlight (Spring 2022), Ukraine in the work of international poets (2022), Welcome to Britain Anthology (Civic Leicester, 2023), Voices Israel Poetry Anthology (2023), The Cannon's Mouth (2024), The Littoral Literary Magazine (2024). His short story, 'Brushing Shoulders with Andrzej Wajda,' was published in in honour of the artist (Mickiewicz, ed., 2018). He is on the editorial committee of Exiled Ink, devoted to works by refugee and migrant writers in Britain.

A Day in Crete

Early morning,

Shrouded in mist, distant hills rise from the water,

as sun sweeps across the horizon.

Fishing boats approach the harbour,

gliding confidently back home.

9 a.m.

A flock of geese, the harbour's mascots,

take an early morning swim,

then climb back on the rock again,

awaiting left-overs from the fishermen's catch.

Afternoon Coffee Break

We sit and order coffee, some cake,

maybe even a complimentary glass of raki.

I love sitting there in squares and cafes,

under Mediterranean sky.

Old Venetian Harbour

Pink domed mosque by setting sun,

last sunrays stroking, caressing city walls.

White stoned lighthouse proudly gleaming,

as passersby stroll along cobbled stones.

What can you hear?

I love singing in a choir.

The sound that pours out from us

lifts up my spirits each week.

Garden birds in the morning

sing full-throated melodies,

sometimes with call and response.

At first, robins and blackbirds

greet the new day as the sun

reaches low bush and branches.

Then, cooing of wood pigeons,

followed by cawing of crows

found in higher up branches.

I find my own voice through song

and reading my poems at

open mic sessions in pubs.

David Lee Morgan

Haiti

Now that was a revolution

When they told us about it in school

I imagined it was an overnight affair

Suddenly, the slaves rise up and slaughter the masters

Good riddance to bad trash, but it wasn't like that, no

It was twelve long years of bloody civil war

Haiti

In all the Americas, from the Boston Tea Party to Simon Bolivar

You were something different, something more, beyond
independence

Revolution

Made by slaves

To end slavery

And you won

They will never forgive you for this

They will never forgive you for being free

And we will never forget

What they did to you

What they're doing to you now

What they're doing to the entire planet

Haiti

You were the perfect storm

The explosive combination

Of high mountains and wide plains

Fresh running rivers and tropical rain

Trade winds and ocean currents

You were the internet of the colonial world

Sailors and slaves

Sweating on the docks

The music of many languages

The sun beats down

The ships come and go

And the word sails out across the ocean

Liverpool, Manchester, the Kingdoms of Africa

The French Revolution, Cap Français

You were the tip of the triangle

The first port of call for the slave trade

The pearl of great price that the monsters fought to own

The richest colony the world had ever known

Back in the days when sugar was spun into liquid gold

Why is sugar so sweet

Maybe it's the blood that makes it so

The cane stalks that cut you like knives

The stripping machines that tear off limbs

The vats of boiling syrup

The fumes that kill you at a distance

The whips and machetes that do it up close

Maybe it's the blood soaked soil

Maybe it's the ghost haunted wind

The silent howls of the island's first people

Who greeted Columbus with festivals

And were paid back with annihilation

Haiti

You were the voice of Africa, singing to the wind ghosts

You were the stolen seeds, carried away on slave ships

Rooted in Africa, but rising up in the New World

Seven short years – they consumed you so quickly

Cheaper to work you to death and bring in fresh

So that's what they did

And that was their mistake

Too many Africans

Too many warriors trained in battle

What if you were born enslaved

You still have freedom in your bones

Maybe you lack the skills of battle

Lack a vision of what could be

Kept in ignorance, killed if you learn to read

But maybe you hear stories in the market

You hear about kingdoms across the ocean

And imagine – what if you grew up in a powerful kingdom

What if you fought in a war, were captured and sold as a slave

What if you were strong enough to survive the middle passage

And then you were sold into the field and the sugar refinery

Seven years is a long, long time to be dying day by day

Maybe it's time enough to plan an insurrection

Maybe it's time enough to start a war

When I was a young revolutionary

I read a quote from Mao Tse-tung

A revolution is not a dinner party, or writing an essay, or painting a
picture, or doing embroidery; it cannot be so refined, so leisurely
and genteel, so temperate, courteous, kind, restrained and
magnanimous. A revolution is an insurrection, an act of violence
by which one class overthrows another.

Mao said it

I read it

And I understood it

But I didn't get it

Buried deep in my imagination was a vision of us, the
revolutionaries

Arm in arm with the masses in their hundreds of millions

Marching on the capitalist class and their pitiful lackeys

Easy to laugh at this now

Back then, revolution was on the rise

Now it's fascism

Now we can see and feel in our gut the terrible threat

But that's what makes the sugar sweet

Not the pain and the suffering but the possibility of deliverance

We are blessed and cursed by necessity

We can make a new world

We must

The old one is dying

Ancestor Worship

There is one essential requirement for being an ancestor

You must be dead

But if you're dead, you can't be anything, because you're not there

You don't exist

Some would say, "You exist in the memories of those you left
behind"

No

The memories exist, but you are gone

You're not an actor

You're not an agent

Any effect you could have had on the material world

Has already been set in motion

Maybe you were a big noise when you were alive

Maybe the noise you made echoes down through the centuries

In books, in stories, in video and computer games

Or maybe you were a nobody

Maybe you were forgotten almost as soon as you died

Or even before

No matter what, you are not a you anymore

You have melted into the music of the universe

The story is told that one long winter night

The shadow just outside the campfire light

Found Finn MacCool, staring into the flames

Tell me, said the shadow

What is the most beautiful music in the world?

And Finn replied

The most beautiful music in the world is the music of what
happens

That's you, what you are, what we all are

A magical wave in an endless magical ocean

And you are not limited by who was your daddy

Or your mother

Or your father's mother's uncle's cousin's brother

You are the child of every ripple in the universe

Who are your ancestors?

That's up to you

Choose wisely

I choose Spartacus

And Mary Magdalene

And Harriet Tubman

And Sapho

And Malcolm X

And William Shakespeare

And I choose you

I know you're not dead yet

But I choose all the ghosts bubbling up inside you

The magic of the universe

Coming out through your lips

Kissing me, breathing into me

Making me love you

I choose you

Description

These two poems are taken from UNCLE TOM'S WAR: Haiti and the Whipping Machine (published by Bidrohi Books https://bidrohibooks.com/). It's the story of the Haitian Revolution (1791-1804) in the context of the American and French Revolutions, the war against slavery and the rise of Fascism in the modern world.

Eleanor Chiari

Introduction

Eleanor has been writing poetry for five years but had never performed at a poetry open night until her inaugural performance at Creative Souls in Balham in June 2025. Eleanor teaches at university and is a part-time Unitarian Lay Pastor.

Forgotten Ancestors

Oh, unknown and unknowable ancestor
you who once walked this earth
with the same uncertain steps as I take,
in the conscious space between memory and dream,
just trying to survive.

We sit in the shade of your trees
Kept alive from birth by institutions you helped make possible.

The national health service,
The eight-hour working day,
the right to vote,
the right to love,
did not come to us without your suffering in almshouses,
on picket lines or in prisons.

I thank you for the more intangible things too:
the idea of the common good,
the dignity of all people,
a sense of the possibility of a loving God
or the freedom to have no God at all.

And all those other things I take for granted:
the sewers and the electric grid.
eyeglasses and C-sections.
controlling the heat of a room
by the soft click of a plastic dial.

I may not know you
daughter of the plague,

son of Omaha Beach,
sister of the carefully planned lesson.
I may not know you
brother of the blueprint,
father of melodies hummed on ships,
in cotton fields and cathedrals.

I may not know you
yet your sweat built my cities,
your grief changed my laws,
your creativity birthed every note
and every brushstroke
that make this world a little more bearable

Not just for me, but for every human
since we joined the community
back in the beginning of the world.

Flying Salamander Dreams

I like to think amphibians have deep spiritual lives
when their black eyes stare over the surface water
and reflections tighten around their chins.

They're thinking of Shiva
or the Madonna of Montserrat.

Don't be distracted by their bubbles and croaks.
Hasty Western biologists mistake them
for mere mating calls.

They are chanting the Gayatri mantra
or searching for the fifth note
in the symphony of the universe.

Late at night, up in the mountains
you hear it too. That subtle rumble
coal train humming along your spine.

Let yourself float across air and landscape
beyond planets and ailing stars
then stretch your limbs wide across the dewy grass
and breathe in your life.

Frank Bolaji Irawo

Introduction

Frank is a coach, speaker and published poet with over 30 years of leadership experience working in Retail, Entertainment, Banking, Criminal Justice and Not-For-Profit sectors. He is passionate about supporting leaders to make a positive impact through their work without compromising their wellbeing or that of the planet. He harnesses the power of words to awaken insight and open doors of awareness that initiate transformation. His unique coaching approach uses poetry as part of powerful transformative conversations that fuse human psychology, neuroscience, and mindfulness to help leaders get clear on who they are, connect to themselves and their mission, and collaborate with the universe to create positive change in their world.

His book DREAM (ISBN: 1913905667) showcases his unique coaching approach using poetry as part of powerful transformative conversations.

He harnesses the power of words to awaken insight and open doors of awareness that initiate transformation.

Woo Woo

Way **O**ver **O**rdinary

Out way over there

On beyond realms of reason

Be wary, beware

Don't get caught

Avoid the swamp

I'm so concerned

I'll say it twice

Mind all that

Woo woo cr*p

Whimsy as it is woolly

Beyond the grasp

Of what can be measured

That which Newtonian science

Turns its nose up at

Out into the realms

Of "spirituality"

That's what it seems

God help us

Religion has no part in this

Hate to get caught in that loop

Entrapped in an illusory world

Of my own making

Only interested in numbers

I can crunch

These ideas and notions

So beyond what I can touch

Do nothing but make me nervous

What good will any of it

Do me

Living in the realms of reality

Woo woo has no real appeal

We look, we see

But do we really?

Science of the

Quantum kind reveals

We see as we expect

The illusion of solidity

Formed from waves

Nothing is quite as it seems

The more we look the less we see

The more we seek, the less we find

The more we think we know

The more there is to discover

There are more questions than

There are answers

The things that matter most

Are harder to pin down

The essence of who we are

Can't be captured in a jar

We get the brain

But where is the mind?

Everything held

In intelligent design

Beware the one

Who has it all

Figured out

Better be open

To not knowing

Take delight in mystery

It's where adventures lie

Maybe one day

We'll figure it out

Woo woo may not be

So abstract after all

Most of it persisting

For millions of years

Ancients used different words

An array of metaphors

To point to infinite source

But then maybe we won't

Figure it out

So we are left with just

The joy of the ride

Description

In my work as a transFLOWmation coach, I help people create space between themselves and their thoughts, allowing them to reconnect with their essence and surroundings. I use poetry as a reflective tool for my clients to access deeper understanding, blending words and nature's wisdom to help people experience personal transformation.

The poem reflects on the notion carried by some that any mention of any intelligence beyond left brain intellect is woo-woo. A term phrased to dismiss wisdom passed down through several millennia. Science is beginning to catch up with this kind of wisdom. This is an invitation to remain open to the efficacy of that which we are unable to currently explain.

One

I am the waves at high tide

Clashing into the shore

Sweeping all before me

Who dares stand before me

Better be ready to feel the force

I am the waves at low tide

Sloshing in with a whimper

Washing over those at rest

Embracing all who stand before me

Soothing comfort for those who wade in

I am the depths of the ocean

Neither coming nor going

Home to all creatures large or small

Wearing the waves like hair

The mainstay for all who seek stability

Holding space for all who call it home

I am the cloud that covers the sun

I am the one who weeps upon the earth

Feeding the ocean

To fuel the waves and the depths beneath

I am the space between the clouds and the ocean

I am the conduit of everything

Through me vapours rise and condensation falls

I am the seen and the unseen

All matter and the spaces that make them

The known and the yet unknown

The realised and future infinite possibilities

You, me and everyone else

We are it, and it is we

The only one there is

A lot of the aggression and discrimination going on in the world can be traced back to people split into us and them camps facing off against each other under the notion of a threat to their well-being.

The poem is positioned to present the case for unity from diversity by leveraging the metaphor of water that can show up in different forms and states while never losing its identity as water. My hope is that we would start to see our shared humanity as the overriding banner under which we all stand.

Hugh Bearryman

Introduction

I have been writing poetry since my schooldays, when it became part of my English homework. Since then, I have jotted down bits of doggerel which suddenly appear in my head, turning some of it into longer pieces. I write about myself, my thoughts, and my experiences throughout my life. I write from observation of others and their lives. I write randomly from being inspired by something out of the blue! Sometimes it is serious, sometimes painful, sometimes humorous, but always from the heart. I am semi-retired, having run several small businesses for the last 40 years. I have never enjoyed the best of health, but that in itself has given me a different perspective and served to inform some of my work. I love wordplay, and being able to turn words into something more fulfilling brings me contentment.

One Man's Scream

Why can't anybody hear me?

I'm screaming from the bottom

Of my lungs, but obviously

All they can hear is silence.

Maybe the odd whisper….

Perhaps they imagined it,

For people do imagine.

Tears run down my face:

Is it the strain of shouting

Or the pain of being ignored?

Can they not hear me?

Or just that they won't listen.

13th May 2006

Katelios (Cephalonia)

Wind

Rain wet, wind roaring,

Soaring up the valley;

Kicking up the brown leaves,

Picking off the green leaves.

Creaking gates, whipping ponds,

Gust low,

Gust slow,

Gusting fast,

Rushing past the tops of trees.

Now a whimper, then a sneeze.

Autumn 1982

Jahki Todd

Introduction

Jahki is an emerging poet with a deep love for the classics, drawing inspiration from literary greats such as John Keats and William Wordsworth. Her poetry often explores themes of life and nature, weaving vivid imagery and thoughtful metaphors to capture the beauty and complexity of existence.

A lover of language in all its forms, she is particularly drawn to the poetic richness found in the Bible, especially in the books of the prophets, where metaphor and symbolism breathe life into timeless messages. Her writing reflects a reverence for the artistry of words, shaped by both classic and sacred influences.

Outside of poetry, she enjoys crocheting, Scrabble, and all types of word games, finding joy in both creativity and the playful precision of language. With a fondness for cats and quiet moments, her poetry often carries a reflective tone, balancing warmth with introspection.

As a fairly new poet, she is just beginning to share her work with the world, stepping into the space of public poetry with curiosity and passion. Her writing continues to evolve as she explores new ideas, refines her voice, and connects with readers who appreciate the lyrical beauty of words. She has self-published a book of poems titled: Kaleidoscope of Life which can be purchased from Amazon Books.

Earthing

Between God's blue heaven

And His blessed green earth

I live and breathe in

The stagnant air

Putrid with man's ugly inhumanity;

Walk the cemented silvery jungle

Adorned in glass veils.

Among the wandering solemn beasts

Quieted by life's struggles,

The Human Race

Rush back and forth

Performing rites of life,

Living their days

Pouncing between changing blades of strife and calm.

I savour the ethereal bounties

Swift and fleeting

Beneath the ever-changing skies

Mostly black or gloomy grey

Sometimes blue sprinkled with white;

I bask in a moment

Absorbing the warmth

Endowed by a distant star

But hide, unsettled

By its hydrous benedictions;

I journey through these concrete forests

Stiff and unforgiving

As the pervading circumstances,

Plodding paths

Of ordered, rigid, grey pavestones

Dappled with the remnants

Of a rubbery feast

Pressed firmly into the teeth-like grips

To form a spotted grey pattern

Like my polka dot dress

Worn for Sunday mass.

And still, I thank God

For I have life.

<u>Description</u>

EARTHING - life as a meditation on existence—the tension between the natural world and the rigid structures we build around ourselves. Our existence carries with it the weight of humanity's flaws. The city, in all its towering coldness, is both a habitat and a cage, where we move endlessly in the rites of survival.

The poem reflects my experience of life's dualities—the fleeting beauty of nature against the grey monotony of the streets and buildings. I watch the sky shift, mostly heavy and dark, but occasionally breaking into blue. I cherish the sun's warmth for a moment, like the good things in life, but when the rain comes, it unsettles me, like life's uncertainties.

Even the simplest details, like the dirty pavement beneath my feet, remind me of the small patterns of daily life. The gum pressed into stone takes me back to the polka-dot dress I wear to church, contrasting the ugliness of the mundane with the beauty of a garment worn to worship God. Life is relentless, rigid, sometimes suffocating—but in all of it, I am still finding beauty, and I am grateful that God has blessed me with life.

Unbroken Ties

I bear with loathing

My ancestors' pain:

Wear it

A heavy chain around my neck

Descending with brutal elegance

To shackle my feet

Invisible and intense;

Intrinsically etched

And embellished

With the wickedness

Of tyrannical masters long dead,

Alive in my bones and cells.

I cry out for emancipation

Plead for freedom

But only in my head.

Silence.

Every attempt to break

These accursed bonds

Binds it tighter

A knot that won't be loosed:

It is in my lifeblood

Flowing in my veins

A foreboding, haunting emotion

Polluting my essence

Woven in my flesh

A calloused reminder in my skin

I cannot dig it out

Intransigence.

My wounded heart pounds

Anger and hopelessness

Shoot Upward to fill my ears, my head

Barbaric, merciless deeds

Perpetrated by

Wicked white devils,

Who call us uncivilised beasts,

Masquerading as gentlemen.

I bear with loathing

my ancestors' pain

Wear it

a gilded yoke around my neck.

Description

When I wrote this poem, I wanted to capture the weight of slave history—the kind of pain that doesn't fade with time but instead embeds itself in the body, passed down through generations. This is about inherited trauma, the suffering of my ancestors that I cannot shake. According to psychologists, our ancestors' trauma is woven into our DNA. It is not just a memory, but a presence, etched into my very being. And which can't be forgotten because racist behaviours still persist even now.

The chains and shackles in the poem aren't physical, but they feel just as real, and it also speaks of the continuing discrimination we face in society today. They descend with "brutal elegance," meaning they have been imposed upon me so seamlessly that they have become part of my identity. No matter how much I cry out for emancipation, that cry exists only in my head. I cannot escape. Every attempt to pull away only tightens the knot, a suffocating cycle that refuses to loosen.

The blood imagery is intentional—it's in my veins, in my flesh, woven into my skin itself. That signifies how oppression and its effects live within me and still continue even now. It's something I cannot simply shed or forget, and the oppressors have woven that into societal norms and behaviours in a clandestine way. Even my calloused skin serves as a reminder of past wounds, history's grip on the present.

And then there's the anger. There is no hesitation when I name those responsible: "wicked white devils" masquerading as gentlemen. That line calls out the hypocrisy of those who inflicted suffering while presenting themselves as civilised. They deemed us uncivilised beasts while committing barbaric, merciless acts against us. I wanted to make sure that contradiction was clear— that their so-called civility was just another mask for cruelty.

By repeating the opening lines at the end, I reinforce that this pain is cyclical. I bear my ancestors' suffering from beginning to end. Though the chain transforms into a "gilded yoke," meaning the oppression has changed form, it has not disappeared—it is still there, shaping my reality.

This poem is a reckoning. It is grief. It is rage. It is a refusal to forget. And it is the undeniable truth that history's wounds don't vanish—they persist, shaping the present, flowing through our blood, embedded in our bones.

James McKenzie

Introduction

James is revisiting poetry he wrote many years ago, and the process has been cathartic and has inspired him to explore his creative muse again.

Frozen in Time Silver Moon

See our fractured soul scattered beneath the clouds.

I feel my soul buried deep beneath the frozen tundra.

The ice is vivid, cold against my being.

I want only to reach outwards, feel my fingers sweeping through
the air.

Time reveals nothing. Not longitude nor latitude. Not space nor
freeness of movement.

I want for nothing. Maybe only to reach outwards and to recover
and then recover again whilst frozen in time beneath the sky.

Then I was watching you… as you swam into the blue.

Watching you… as you performed your breathing trick.

And you swam into the blue and you dived into the deep, dark
blue.

And you stayed down there. Oh, it seemed just like a lifetime.

And she said:

I will show you how. I will bring you down. Then I will take you
out to see the most, the most silver moon 🌙 🌙 🌚

Frozen in Time Silver Moon was made up of the lyrics to a song I wrote and a poem, and has existential and esoteric themes on life and the human condition.

The Drifting

So why, somehow, the drifting

Those things we kept, she is listening

To the water's edge at our shore

To the flowers that watch the eagle soar

Their petals lay all around

They scream and shout, yet make no sound

If bark is wood, then skin must be

The lining of this tree that's me

And now this water I have found

I drink it in, and I feel so drowned

Fire is liquid; it dances

Its smoke delivers me clearly

I feel their love surround me

I feel her love so dearly.

___Description___

The Drifting is a poem about loss, bereavement, and ultimately, hope for new beginnings.

James Smith

Introduction

An acute sense of place and an eye for the telling detail infuse James A. Smith's writing, whether in poetry, lyrics or prose. James has had a long and varied creative life, reaching back to teenage poetry performances in the early 1970s, through folk clubs, rock bands and electronic music in the 80s and 90s, DJ-ing, and more bands in the 21st century. More recently, he returned to his first love, spoken word, fertile ground that recently produced his first published volume of verse, 'I Saw Michael Caine.'

Village Hall Disco, North Waltham, 1971

It was the night I discovered Al Green
Because I was 'so tired of being alone;
so tired of on my own,' too
I chatted up the deejay
To ask him who was singing
With that voice drenched in honey
Or an undiscovered shade of deepest blue

The deejay was godlike behind his double-deck console
But he deigned to speak to me, an ignorant teenage arsehole
And he educated me just enough
That I could call my friend's bluff
And pretend I had full knowledge
By knowing the essential stuff

It was also the night I asked a pretty girl to dance
It took an eternity to screw up the nerve
My eyes entranced
By her tempting curves
Surely, I had half a chance
My hair was clean, my shirt bright yellow
I was tall, and shy, and acne-free,
A callow, hopeful fellow

Was I a fool or a bright young dreamer?
Was I heading for love?
Or a sad misdemeanour?
I smoothed my kipper tie and clenched my fists
Thought of lips I longed to kiss…
'Would you like to dance with me?

Take a chance with me?'
That's all I had to say

But courage lacked at first, and fear stepped in
I was still too young for the crutch of whiskey or gin
Half a bitter shandy was my only helper
Until, at last, I danced up close
And with a spurt of daring,
The vital words were blurted out
Emerging, however, in an over-loud shout
That found an unfortunate quiet pause between the hits
And mutated into a broken yelp, reeking of despair
For everyone to hear, and laugh and stare
At me, and my heart in a million bits
Before the lines had faded in that humid, treacherous air

I fled to the gents, trying not to cry
And smoked an underage cigarette
My head seething with shame and deep regret
And resolved that it would be the last time that I would try
Such foolishness,
Forever, or until the village hall burned to the ground
And my martyred bones were found,
Bleached by fire
In a distant mythic future,
By kindly archaeologists, of unfulfilled desire.

London, 2024

<u>***Description***</u>

An advantage of age is being able to laugh at many of the things that mortified you in your teens. I grew up in rural Hampshire, but the village disc was as fraught with pitfalls as any big city club.

Before Your Light Turned Dark

A beach in my memory,
not the Isle of Wight, in the 1960s
Where my childhood holidays had begun
But later, two decades later,
A long white beach in Plakias, Crete, 1981

David and Lisa sitting in the doorway
of David's tent.
I met them yesterday.
He's a handsome Canadian, a few years older than me.
She's about my age, sleek and golden, and with a German accent.
The grape seller has just been by,
Refusing to bargain,

Though we have to try.

A perfect afternoon edging towards its conclusion,
Squinting into the westering sun, glory-bound
Soon to submerge behind the evening mountain,
Dazzling my enraptured gaze,
And when it disappears, you make a silly popping sound
And we dissolve into laughter
The warmth between us in my heart forever after

Flip forward in time, thirty-five years.
And David is my best friend, and he's dying,
I know, because he told me weeks ago
And I have seen him with my own eyes,
And I held him, skin and bone, in my arms.
When I came to Vancouver, to say my goodbyes

And we've known love since day one
So we could even laugh
At the truth of your coming death
As we always laughed
As if laughter was our version of breath

Even at the last moment, we joked,
Before I walked away, drove away,
Eyes filling so fast, I had to park
Out of sight, down the road
And let the tears flow
And then I flew home
Not long before your light turned dark.

And soon you weren't there,
Or here
Or anywhere
And I still don't like _it_

Not one
Little
Bit!

Description

Finding a photograph in a bundle of mementoes was the trigger for
this poem. Losing friends is one of the saddest things in any kind
of life, long or short, and David deserved a suitable memorial for
his wonderful life.

Jermaine Crockett

Introduction

Jermaine Crockett was born in America but moved to England at a young age. He writes about the world we live in and past experiences. He started writing poems at the age of 18 and then moved on to spoken word at age 20.

Penny for Your Thoughts

Due to inflation, it's no longer a penny for my thoughts

It's £1.50

Plus, a service fee

Plus, VAT

So altogether, that's £2.50

And I said please because manners don't cost anything, and I'm smiling while saying this, so that's a service with a smile.

Which is pretty rare these days. I'm guessing you haven't seen a smile in a while.

Due to the prices going up, it's no longer a penny for my thoughts

It's £1.50

Plus, I give my thoughts in poetry

So that's an extra fee.

Plus, I don't know what I'm thinking these days

For days, my brain is caught up in a daze

Trapped in a maze

But never amaze

On how my money always splits ways.

Due to the inflation and the cost of living, a penny for my thoughts

It's £1.50

Plus, service fee

Plus, VAT

Plus, I give my thoughts in poetry

So, altogether, we looking at £5.80.

But growing up, I would listen to my mum sing to Luther
Vandross and Janet Jackson; the best in life are free.

I believe poetry and the beauty of thinking are two of the best
things in life.

So don't you worry, ladies and gentlemen, my thoughts and poetry
are a gift to you. You can have this for free.

This Drink

This drink is called Budweiser

But every sip just makes me dumber

But I still love her

But I often find myself cheating on her with her Mexican
stepsister, Corona.

She goes well with a slice of lime

She and I always have a good time

And some nights she is by my side when I write my rhymes

She has a sister from Mexico.

Love to speed things up, never takes it slow

She is always ready to go

Her name is Tequlia

With her, it's smile all round

If any shots get in her way, we line them up to knock down

But some days I like to take it easy

With my uncle Jack; last name Daniels

He from Tennessee

He original - no apple, no honey, just pure whisky.

Joanna Bergin

Introduction

I have always loved poetry, and writing and reading it have helped me through some of the hardest times in my life!

For the last nine years, I have been reading my poems at a private poetry salon and am now working on putting some of them together to publish a book, as well as recording them. I am also a classical singer and one of my poems (which I have yet to read at Creative Souls) has been turned into a song, written for me by the wonderful Finnish composer called Olli Mustonen, as a surprise birthday present. It was commissioned by the inimitable Steven Isserlis to whom I am incredibly grateful and will be published by Schott after I have given the premiere. Apart from that, I had a tiny little poem read on "Quote Unquote" (also by the latter!) on BBC Radio 4 during the pandemic called "Corona Hope."

Sacred

When your (my) heart turns this way and that,
When you (I) try to sabotage everything.
"That's right, go on, throw it all away."
Because you are scared.
Just to provoke a reaction?
Nothing more,
Nothing less.
That is what it is all about.
The cowering little child inside you
Scared.
And, at the same time, SACRED.
So next time you are scared,
Possibly because you are scarred,
Just remember that one thing, my love,
YOU ARE SACRED!
A shaft of light and good,
And nothing more
Needs to be said or even understood.
We must all honour this in each other.
YOU-ARE-SACRED!!!
WE-ARE-SACRED!!!

<u>Description</u>

I wrote this poem to encourage and remind both other people and
myself not to self-sabotage, because we are SACRED!

PRISM

On the surface,

The colours of my body are

Mostly a subtle affair,

A gentle blending of skin

And hair.

Very pale pinks

A few greenish blue lines,

Tend to be what I see when

I look down

With my very blue eyes

My head inclined

Covered mostly in light brown hair.

A few nuances here and there.

Then we go in deeper,

In there

The colours are

More pronounced;

Red blood rushing

Through it all.

Different textures

Making up my different bits,

Some squishy squashy

And others, more spongy.

These extraordinary

Robust but so sensitive

Machines,

Which permit me

To create,

To connect,

To caress…

My friends

They come in many hues,

But inside out

We could easily be confused!

And to what purpose

Do these temples exist?

Why, to house the most precious

And a vibrant gift of all:

Our soul!

From here shines out every colour

of the rainbow;

Every shade from orange to indigo,

Red, yellow, green, blue,

And plenty more;

Revealing our feelings

And painting our mood.

Our senses

Are prisms, too;

Our eyes and ears

Inviting in images and sounds

That sing and dance around,

While feeding our souls

Which thrive on such magic

Creating alchemy when cajoled.

And I know for sure

That whatever our outside shade or tint,

Our insides match,

And if we truly listen,

Our hearts will always see

Each other

In full, rich, glorious colour.

Description

This one I wrote for a competition where the theme was something to do with "colour, identity and the body."

Julia Young

Soon it will be spring

Soon, the goslings will hatch and

make thin trails on the lake and

the mud will grow shallow and

green things will sprout abundant.

Soon, the air will be warmer and

larvae buried deep will emerge and

break upwards from pupae to fly and

we'll swat them from our ankles, laughing.

Soon, the sleeping buds will wake and

snowdrops and daffodils will burst and

our ungloved hands will swing soft and

we'll undress our winter selves and

the trees will put on their summer clothes.

Soon, the brown pools on paths will linger less and

be rebirthed as solid ground and

little ones will throw off their shoes and

run wild through new shoots of grass

Soon, the weight of leaves and

bluer skies and

lost sunglasses and

changing seasons will hang

pregnant in the air and

soon, it will be spring.

By the Cam

Sometimes I feel the light stretch through me.

Feel the feet of people past press up into mine,

forty or four hundred years apart,

those who used to live hard and live young,

looking up at the same milk-yellow sun.

Sometimes I hear time sweep soft beside me,

Hear the whisp of a breeze of a thought,

of a Solution or conclusion,

a subtraction or intrusion.

Of original creation, the present becoming history,

The storied becoming story.

Khalilah Ismaiel - Empress Khalilah

Introduction

My name is Empress Khalilah. I am a mother, grandmother, teacher, African drum facilitator, poetess, lover and more.

Stand and Stare

We have no time to stand and stare. Is it because we really don't care?

Nature's first green is a golden sight to be seen, as she unfolds.

Nature is the anchor and the first seed of what we need to feel.

The sun shining so brightly, convening warmth for everyone; go get some!

The silvery, perfectly round, comes out with no sound.

The symbolic entities of the stars seem so far, with dazzling constellations on par.

Then, there's the sky, go spread your wings, it's time to fly.

Look at the birds singing high in the treetop allies, look at the squirrels rustling through the grass, having a blast.

The beauty of nature, a creative, uncontrollable source in the galactic university of life.

The beauty of nature is what we are; yet, it seems so far.

So, let's find time to stand and stare with our feet bare, because we really do care.

Description

This poem came to my thoughts as I sat on a bench in a park. I observed people rushing by at speed either going to work or taking children to school. I remember wishing I had a magic wand to stop everyone in their tracks and say. Let's stop and stare at the beauty that nature has given to us.

"Nature is not a place to visit, its home." – Gary Synder

Pagan

Pagan, pagan, pagan
You tink seh we done
You tink seh we done
We jus ah come
We jus ah come.

From the ancient monarchy of Timbuktu, you have no clue what
we have been through
You despised, chastised and tyrannised our people; we broke the
chains of slavery.

Pagan, pagan, pagan
You tink seh we done
You tink seh we done
We jus ah come
We jus ah come.

We don't care who you are, we don't care where you're from, oh
Jah is here with I, and I high up in Mount Zion, we hail Rastafari.

We have the ancient ancestral African drums entrusted to us from
the Malian empire, completed.
We will not be defeated.

We broke the chains of his story.

We are blacknificent Africans from the highlands of Ethiopia to
the shores of Senegal.

We are blacknificent Africans from the heart of Congo to the
deserts of Namibia.

We are Africans; we got our features and our names from her.
Mama Africa.

Description

Approximately 12.5 million enslaved Africans were captured and
transported across the Atlantic over the course of the transatlantic
slave trade.

This poem was inspired by the evil atrocities in Africa, from the
transatlantic slave trade to the hidden hand of imperialism, the
destruction of African armies to the weaponisation of terrorism.

"If there is no struggle, there is no peace." – Federick Douglas

Larusta

Introduction

Larusta is a London-based songwriter and singer who also writes poetry.

His debut album, 'The Life You Save May Be Your Own,' was released in autumn 2024, praised by NOTION magazine for its "evocative storytelling and haunting melodies." His songs, revolving around the human condition, start out, more often than not, as poems. He is currently working on his second album while performing solo or with his band 'Larusta & The Dead Dogs' inside and outside of London. The following works represent his latest allusive output.

The Fable of the Rabbit & The Snake

In the meadow of a forest

Lives a rabbit and a snake

The rabbit has only one ear

And he's a gloomy motherfucker

While the snake is mostly a snake

But she is beautiful

And she knows of her beauty

It makes sure she has always enough to eat

And the rabbit ponders all day long

By night, he goes to sleep

When the rabbit had two ears

He found out about the snake

Their paths crossed

The snake was cheerfully smiling

And the rabbit smiled right back

He thought, "What is it about this snake?

I've never seen a snake like that."

Soon, he forgot about her snakeness

And about his rabbithood

The more often he saw the snake

He hoped it would finally be for good

The snake was jovial

She never mentioned her present, nor her past

She discreetly watched the rabbit

Thinking, "How long will this guy last?"

Until the day they met at the snake's dugout

The rabbit thought he knew what it was about

The snake, however, asked him about his latest plunder

The rabbit said, "I'm in the forest not to plunder

I'm here to watch, to run and wonder"

On went the night, and the rabbit replied with bravery

He only thought, "This stubborn snake

Why can't she see the real me?"

In a moment of carelessness

He got too close to the snake

And she bit off his ear

In his eyes, she could see

The pain of 4.5 billion years

Not for his ear, he cried

Or he may perish here

The world cast off its veil

And a dream that dies is a dream to fear
Description

I wrote this one down in a frenzy, urged by a personal story that happened about the time when I played with the band in Berlin in November 2024. There's a pureness to animals which makes them great archetypes.

Wrestle with the Angel

This is the pitiless story

Told as the twilight fails

I hear your deep breathing

As long as strife prevails

You sit by the fire

Not raising a brow

To the arrant desire

Of my here and now

You know the skeletons

I vow not to tame

Or release from the closet

You hold the keys to my aim

I need to wrestle with you

And if you

Pull me into the sky

To let me fall

I'm willing to fall

I need to

Make you squall

If I sing small,

There's no point at all

Do not claim there would be

Ill movements in my brain

When I see you spread your wings

In the wasteful Whitsun rain

For beggars and kings

Who willingly take flight

You tug at benign heartstrings

Insisting you are right

And from the highest ground

You denounce my best miscues

Said and done with worlds to be won

Without a world to lose

I need to wrestle with you

And if you

Pull me into the sky

To let me fall

I'm willing to fall

I need to

Make you squall

If I sing small

There's no point at all

Description

Inspired by the story of Jacob wrestling with the angel in the book of Genesis. The life you want to lead won't be handed to you on a silver platter. You have to fight for it, even if the chance of succeeding is low. What other option do you have? Not trying is like dying before your time.

Luigi Coppala

Introduction

Luigi Coppola – www.LinkTr.ee/LuigiCoppola – poetry, music,
rum and coke. Southbank Centre's New Poets Collective
23/24, Poetry Archive Worldview winner, Bridport Prize shortlist,
Ledbury & National Poetry Competition longlist, he produces
music as 'The Only Emperor' and has a debut collection due
Summer 2025 from Broken Sleep Books.

Mark Shuttleworth in the brambles in the bushes.

The Eyes of Animals

I'm looking through the shop window
at the filled rows, glass boxes and walls.
Did I mention the smell? Was there one?
Yes: it was musk, warmth, dust, alcohol
infusing this high street zoo of frozen frames.
Trim and pimped on quiet pedestals –
from open field, wood, stream to shelved
herd, flock, shoal of distant cousins.

I'm staring at the cow head: its pert ears
pointless satellites; its nose a dried oyster
glued back on slightly off-angle; its eyes,
in their wide blackness reflecting every blade,
fence, muddied machine and that final
hollowing out by prod then pistol.

***

Words by Luigi Coppola;

Art Mark Shuttleworth

Multimedia for the poem here:
www.linktr.ee/TheEyesOfAnimals

String Theory

We settled on string, having tried

and failed to use, among other things:

wood, plastic, fire, bread, talcum powder,

chewable vitamins, meconium, nail clippings,

breath and thoughts about mothers.

First, we pulled apart the strands: an un-

twisting of a Russian doll's hair, every length

identical to the fibre, every width laughing

at the hair on the hands that tugged them free.

We licked each end, as if a thread for

a cosmic needle. We burnt loose wisps

away. We pulled and tugged and jerked

until they could be held erect and parallel

to our feet, quivering at the tension.

Then the real work began. We made shapes

and outlines, tied and twirled until a form

formed in the air: a structure of twine,

a frozen explosion of a ball of wool, mercurial,

morphing, warping in the breeze of our sighs.

That night, we rested in its shadows –

exhausted children in a spider's cradle

with lines of black cast on sweating tan.

It spoke to us in our dreams. We woke

to rope burns on faces, limbs, tight

from this tourniquet of faith – our blood and

our hopes clogging our veins.

***

Words Luigi Coppola, Art Mark Shuttleworth

Multimedia: www.linktr.ee/StringTheoryPoem

Manatita, The Lantern Carrier

Introduction

Manatita, AKA The Lantern Carrier, is a published author and poet who has been performing poetry for 23 years on the London scene.

Equally at home with performance pieces, Lantern Carrier has won a Hammer and Tongue (H&T) Slam, featured at Fire and Dust, Mind Over Matter, Chocolate Poetry, Word Play, Spoken World Online and performed at the famous Nuyorican Cafe. He has been runner-up in Slams, as well as making the finals in the H&T National Final (Brighton). He is a regular in London at Flo Vortex Poetry, run by Natalie Stewart, one of the leading lights in London.

Lantern Carrier is an author and creative writer. He writes essays, plays and Flash Fiction. He is the Author of four books, including Maxims for Our Children: A look at the Teachings of Jesus, the Christ, and Blossoms of the Heart – poetry.

Lantern Carrier is a poet who tries to serve, to bring Light, to elevate… enlighten the understanding. He endeavours to reach the Heart; to bring wisdom to his pieces and is a specialist in nature imagery, music, light, colour and dance in their kaleidoscope of different forms.

All his poetry addresses the varying moods of the soul and the human condition, either in mystical harmony or in separation from its Source. Salaam!

The Magnificent Plateau

Splashes of undulating white, make the ravine

Look even more beautiful! We've seen these

Scenes before, surges of aqua-marine ripples,

Beneath a canopy of blue sky and scattered clouds.

You hold my gaze, a nature lover, watching the

Stream seeping through the magnificent cobbled

Stones, on either side of this stunning canyon.

The verdant hue of the foliage stands regal, enclosed

By glorious grey rock walls, plus an Amphitheatre of

Magical cliffs, dominating the lushness of this plateau.

The harps of minstrels call to me, my Beloved whispering

Melodies to Hearts blending as One, in this breathtaking

Pinnacle-moment… of Being. I gaze upwards,

My soul spilling gratitude, in this dazzling Light of Creation.

Homage to the Light

Love dries the copious tears, spilling from my broken

Dreams –the heaviness of loneliness; the stains of deep

Remorse. Gently, She pats the roses covering the scars

Where thorns once sat, enmeshed in a foliage of desires.

'You've done well,' She whispers: 'The Light that shines

Within, has erased the darkness of a shadowed past.

Arise, my sweet, sweet angel, the brute of past regrets

Shall no more shine, the fragrance of the dawn is gleaming.'

I felt my shoulders breathe. My Heart cried tears of joy,

The soul now laughing with the sun. Love kissed my wounds,

No more the toil of suffering and despair, for I was born anew.

The voice of freedom sang to me, her bird of hope now
perching

On my newfound dreams of Bliss divine, my lack of
expectations.

I bowed, paid homage to the Light, paid homage to the Light.

Mark Rothwell

Introduction

I have always valued the power of words, and in a fast-paced world where we are bombarded with so much information, imagery, text, talking heads, shouting voices, it is easy to speak without thinking, easy to forget the impact words can have.

The weaponising of words in order to crush your opponent.

Poetry: the writing, reading and speaking of carefully chosen words is, for me, an opportunity to pause, to breathe, and to acknowledge the magic moments when we allow ourselves to open up and truly connect with the joy, pain, hope, fear and love that we all feel as humans.

Poetry is one heart talking to another.

The Art of Joinery

Lap

Half lap

Scarfe

Mitre

Hidden Mitre

Dado

Rabbet

Mortise and Tenon

Tusk Tenon

Dovetail

These are names

Of joints

Woodworking joints

Two pieces of wood brought together in a unison of strength

Carved from the heart of an ancient tree

Two independent pieces

Stronger than either can see

Eye, Hand

Pencil, Saw

Hammer, Chisel

You, Me

We come together

Under the hand of a carpenter

This is the art of joinery.

Description

I am a carpenter, and someone asked me if I had ever written a poem about carpentry- I hadn't- so I did.

The Falling Down Man

A man fell down today.

He was standing next to me.

And then, he wasn't

He fell

Soft

Like dropped laundry

Or a coat

Slipped from the back of a chair

He's fallen before

Many times

He was telling us about it

As we stood around

Under a cold sun

Waiting for the guard to unlock the gate

"I fall down a lot," he said

"I have seizures."

And then he fell

A comic's perfect timing

On the ground,

My face close to his,

Searching the glazed egg white eye.

"You're OK?" I say.

A mother's words

In a stranger's mouth

But he doesn't hear me

He's somewhere else

Another country

I kneel

His head

My hand

Cupped against the cold concrete

A mesh bag

Half full

Sits at his feet

A still life

Upright bag

Fallen man

He comes around

Dazed not knowing

I lift him carefully

Like a lover

Or a friend

He is neither

He is old

But not old

Or young

Enough

To fall

As often as he does

In my arms

He is light

My strength wraps around him

Filling the space

Reserved

For a woman or a child

Missing

From the life

Of a falling down man

Upright now

We walk together

Slowly

Under the cold sun

I am with him

But he is not with me

He's somewhere else

Another country

Where the fallen go

After they fall

A place

I hope

Where the sun is not as cold.

Description

Based on a true event that occurred a number of years ago, when I had the misfortune of being incarcerated in Texas.

Martin Howse

Introduction

Martin might be a novice when it comes to poetry, but he has a long history in the music industry, where he's worked for more than 43 years. More used to belting out other people's lyrics in rock bands, at the ripe old age of 60-something, he's rediscovered an interest in the spoken word - proving it's never too late to get into poetry.

Mid-Table Wannabe

My first love was Mandy; she was from Chigwell,

If you don't know, that's Essex – TOWIE central.

I was a Saturday boy, she was a Saturday girl,

And I was besotted, my head in a whirl.

I took her to see Foreigner, but I knew we were through,

When she didn't react to Waiting For A Girl Like You.

It was a time of discovery, of mystery and intrigue,

But I always knew she was out of my league.

Then came Sue; she was from Kent,

Huge 80s hair, like a bloody big tent,

She was the first with whom I had sex,

But not for her – she was shagging her ex.

So that didn't end well, but she remained a good friend,

until aged just 50, cancer got her in the end.

I miss her a lot. She was fun and bubbly,

But one thing was obvious: she was too good for me.

Next, there was Julie, a petite brunette,

One of the nicest women that I've ever met.

We had some laughs, but it lacked the spark,

It kinda fizzled out, and the lights went dark.

But again we're still pals, life's too short to be sore,

And her mum was lovely – I think I liked her more.

Julie married my mate, but that didn't last,

I think I always felt she was out of my class.

And then February '89, we went on a date,

To the Hammersmith Odeon, and in a rare twist of fate,

My car broke down and I couldn't get home,

And since then, I don't sleep alone,

Each morning I wake up and you're there next to me,

And I realise I'm the luckiest man there could be,

Because I'm just ordinary, not bad, but not great.

I'm a mid-table wannabe, punching above his weight.

May 2025

<u>*Description*</u>

Mid-Table Wannabe is a light-hearted tale about never feeling you're quite good enough for your boy or girlfriend. But then finding that magical person who actually realises that you ARE good enough, and making sure that you appreciate that every day. All the names and stories are true.

First-Born Son

I hope that you're proud of the man I've become,

Of the boy that you raised, of your first-born son.

I hope you approve of the choices I've made,

Of the paths that I've travelled, of the battles I've raged.

I hope that you laugh when I mess it all up,

When I fall on my arse, when I act like a chump.

I hope that you smile when you see who I love,

Because she is my world, and if I'm good enough…

… for her, then it's true.

That her love for me is a reflection of you.

I hope that you know that I miss you each day,

How you'd know what to do, how you'd know what to say.

I hope that you're proud of the boy that I've raised,

And can see in my son the foundations you laid.

I wish you were here to see what's become,

Of the boy that you raised, and his first-born son.

March 2025

<u>*Description*</u>

First-Born Son is a letter from a son to his late father. It started out as an autobiographical tale about my own dad, who died when I was just seven years old - but as I was writing it, it evolved into a tale about a man who has a son of their own, and I don't have kids, so the autobiographical element went out the window! But the sentiments remain true.

Massimo Comuzzi

Introduction

Massimo spills his verses like his watercolour art, each stroke
untamed and true, no eraser marks, no second thoughts: Where
love calls, verses follow—Next heartbreak, for tomorrow.

MassimoComuzzi.com

MassimoComuzzi.com

Season of Magic

Ah... Season of magic,

display of mature colours,

A portal to my soul,

A way to feel connected.

I have no master!

I am free to speak!

I am in love with the universe!

Taking off from our bodies

Into glittering energy.

Spacing out..

Coming back..

Your hands fly

and circle,

In harmony,

connecting lives

Your desire is my desire.

In your touch

I relax my heart,

In your flow

I find myself.

Back to myself!

a beauty you forget.

I breathe freedom

like weightless feathers.

Real me,

Shedding identities.

Heart under reconstruction

The universe is so obviously greedy

This needs to be loved

Entirely, completely

I had it once

I had it twice

I want it above all

Ridiculous

It's all about love

Love, Amore

Unearthing with bare hands

Living ink marks on my fingers

Such a killer game,

and when the time of dying comes

Be the river,

always ready.

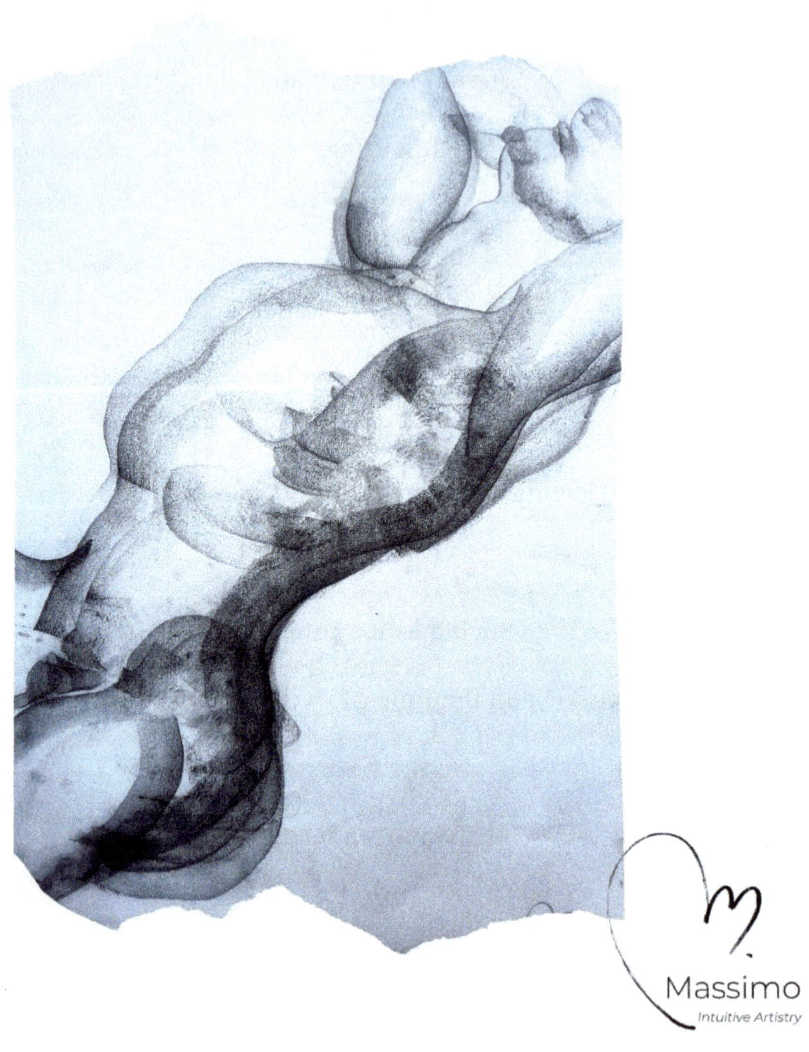

Massimo
Intuitive Artistry

Blue (English and Italian)

In the blue, I get lost

In the blue, I am complete

Home and foreign land

All is known in his hand.

Blue is night

Blue is day

Fluid air.

Deep water

The infinite loop

Blue is where I begin

Blue is where I end

Nel Blu mi perdo

Nel Blue mi completo

Casa e terra straniera

tutto e' conosciuto alla sua maniera

Il blue e' notte

Il blue e' giorno

Aria fluida

Acqua profonda

Il cerchio 'infinito,

Il blue e'dove inizio

e' dove finisco.

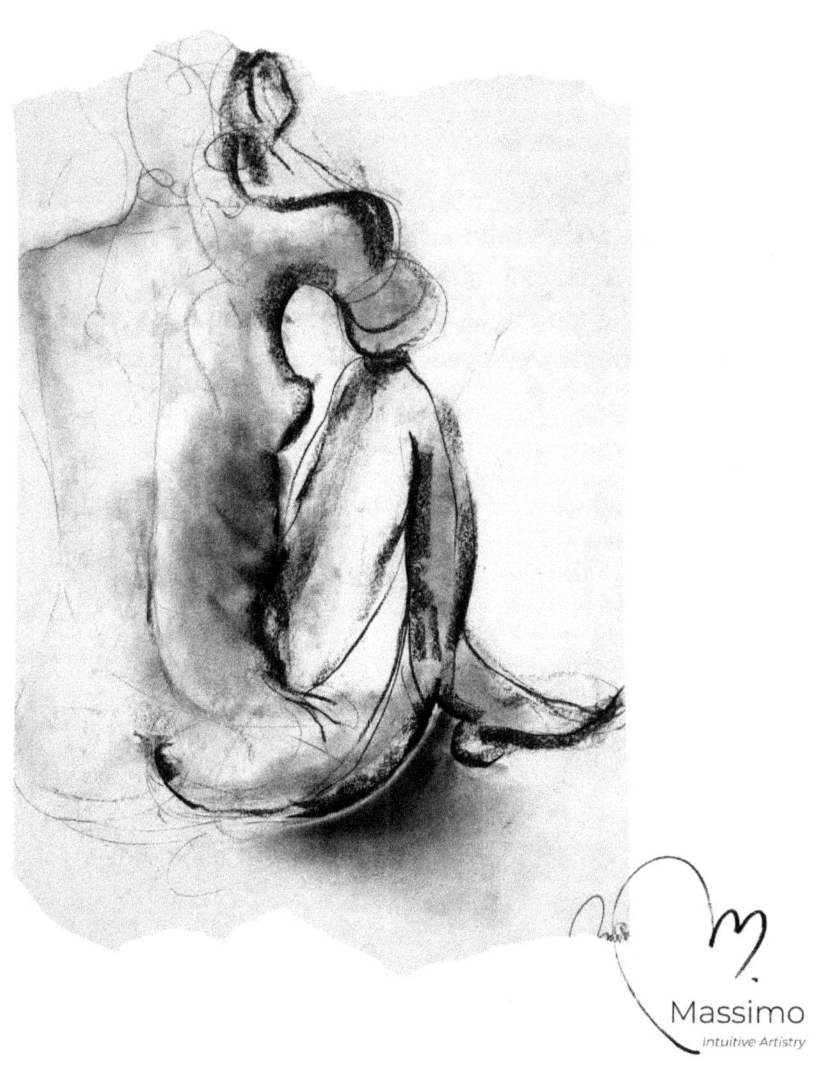

Massimo
Intuitive Artistry

Milena Kamila

Introduction

I started writing poetry while going through a difficult time in my life. Poetry helps me externalise feelings that are often difficult to understand. I like looking at poems I wrote in the past to see how much I have progressed in my understanding of myself and the world.

My Son

I have a son

He is transgender

And then the pause

You all want to be politically correct

Not showing a sign of neglect

Of hypocrisy, since you remember, we live in the country of
democracy

You think you are open-minded

But now you're scared of your thoughts

Tied to your throat with so many knots

And then the question

Always the same one

You think you are so original

To me, you are all so dumb

"Do you accept that?" and "How do you feel about it?"

Not having any idea about the journey and the darkness of the
abyss

I didn't have a choice since my child became invisible and lost
their voice

They couldn't process or express

Life stopped making any sense

Self-harming became the norm

Everything in their room was covered in blood

The school, friends and therapist became unreachable, behind the
thick mist

A fog of confusion, misunderstanding and alienation

Our house was filled with shouting, rude words and accusations

Presented regularly without any hesitation

And the silence, an empty space, the gap

Created between me and my own child

All the professionals so useless, telling me I'm doing really well

Not seeing, every day for me is a living hell

And I had to go to work, since I'm the only provider

What kept me sane, really,

Or maybe running away

a chance to get a couple ciders

And every time I was coming back home, I would stop breathing

Is he still alive?

Or was it his last deep dive?

We both know he cannot thrive.

Even when I'm fully on his side

Once a very talented, hard-working child

Now a shadow, lost soul

And it isn't his fault

Maybe it's mine,

Maybe I should see the signs much earlier and be more supportive

Motherhood can be so distortive

Fast forward, four years later

He is still alive and much better

A drum player, writer, very opinionated, loves history

Stands out from the societal monotony

He proofreads my poems

We talk about gods and deities

And other good and bad omens

So what was your question again?

Do I accept it?

Him being transgender, you mean?

I can only smile, since the air became thin

I can take a deep breath, and it doesn't hurt anymore

And when I leave my house, I can peacefully close the door

And my answer is "I didn't have a choice"

But I wish you wouldn't ever judge him

And I actually have one request

Don't try having opinions about the things you don't understand

Me and you survived a different quest

And even when you can't digest

Just allow things to manifest

Our differences should be celebrated

We are here to be elevated

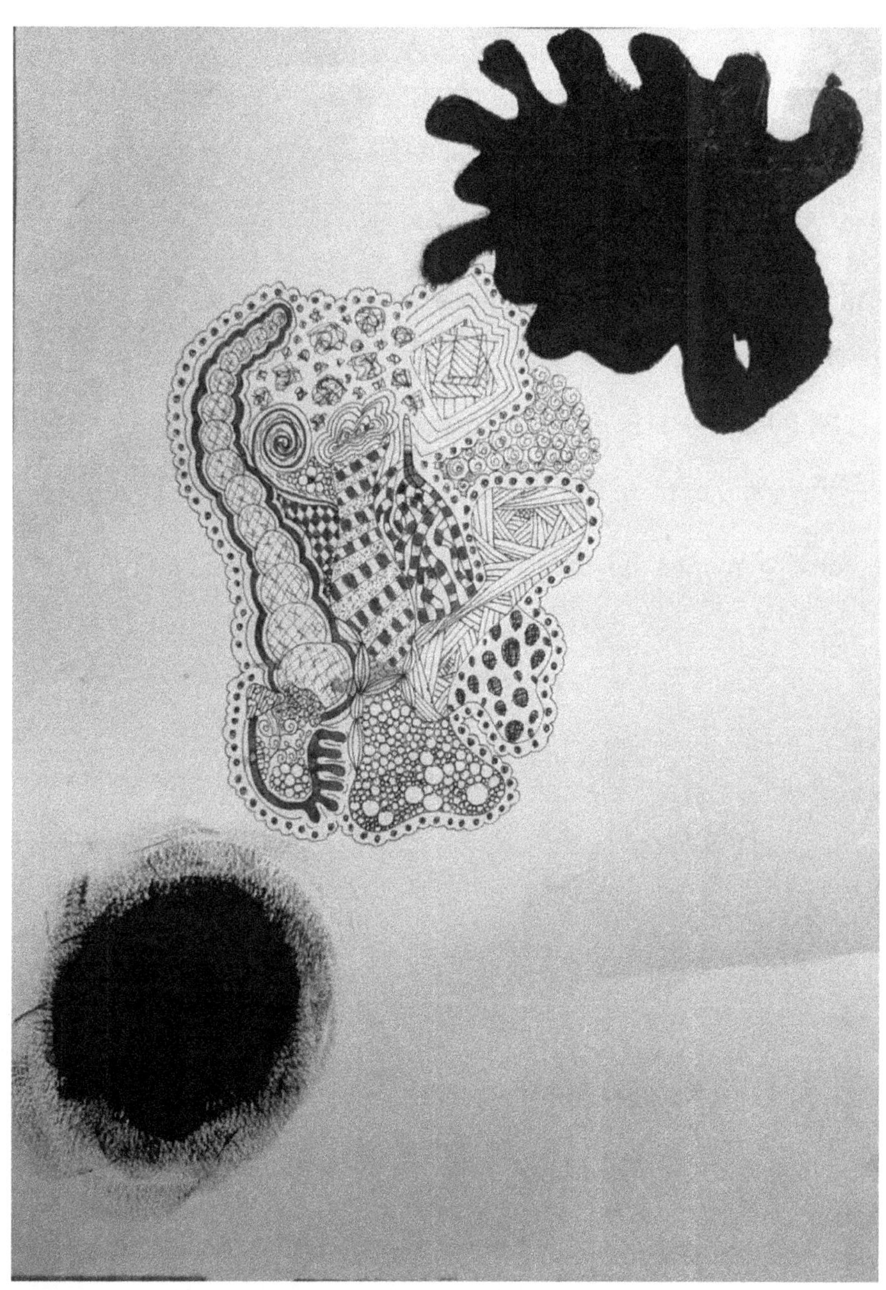

My Superpower

Dear ADHD brain,

They say you're my superpower.

But I cleaned the cooker and the cupboard when I should have just made my breakfast.

Wrapping gifts is an impossible task, but for my mum, it's a must

How can I explain to my grandma that I forgot to call back…?

For two months, just because my thoughts are entangled in train tracks

They say you're my superpower

But object permanence deficit

Will make my bills and letters disappear during my evening shower

Object permanence deficit

You don't exist when out of my reach

Do you know what it does to my mind?

What is my mind trying to teach

My friends, my boyfriend, pfff… disappeared

My heart and my body want to scream,

Feeling like this is just a bad dream

I want to run, but where and actually why?

I will just sit here, and maybe I don't know, cry?

Slow down, breathe…

Even though tonight you won't be able to sleep

And when we argue, or someone makes me angry

I go from 1 to 100, and it can get ugly

And if you try giving some time, giving me space

Because you can see all the emotions on my face

Rejection Sensitive Dysphoria

And don't mistake it for euphoria

For me, that's torture

Difference in brain structure, that's what they say

And you're giving me all the science behind it, you may

But it won't change the fact that I feel different

I feel disabled

Unable to do simple tasks, to follow through

Everything depends on my mood

Dopamine rush and lack

And I really want to scream- O Fuck!

And yes, write essays for hours, as it happened to be my topic

God forbid writing about flowers

And yes, I can talk to anyone easily

But only if it's meaningful, deep, and interesting

Some people's brains at this point are sizzling

They say you're my superpower

Place me in a crisis situation,

you will find a stoic, calm, methodical person

And don't expect me to sit in front of the telly,

For me, it's impossible to grow a big belly

Bicycles, walks, parks, forests

Planning another trip, even when I'm at my lowest

And when I see you, the rest of the world disappears

Hyperfocus

Now my brain is blooming like the flower of the lotus

It took some time to accept myself

My abilities, inabilities, challenges, and strengths

And maybe, one day, I will actually see

My superpower is the only way for me to be

GET SOME
SLEEP
GET SOME SLEEP

Nathaniel Chin

Introduction

I am a poet and creative caught between two worlds, and consider myself a mystic, a dreamer, and a free thinker. I like to write introspective pieces of work, focusing on the human experience, philosophy, inequality, discrimination, racism, empathy, trauma, spirituality, and existential matters.

Evilution

If I'd known of life's pathology,

I'd be reincarnated,

on a distant and lonely world,

where life has barely formed.

Stir up the firmament with lightning,

brimstone and salt for taste,

and chilli flakes to primordial soup.

I'd create a new flavour of existence,

yet who'd appreciate it?

Ambivalent to the planets afar,

first emanations born from a spoken word,

in the form of single cells,

that would turn into single minds,

Because we amoebae do not squalor,

we divide but do not conquer,

all we do is be fruitful and multiply.

Hard to converse without a mouth,

hard to relate when your thoughts aren't your own.

The absence of agency redeemed by an instinct,

to eat, sleep, and procreate,

til we're dead or we're bored.

Dead-bored is what I'll be,

excreted from the annals of the age.

Caught up and concealed,

in a big black hole,

until I could tell the time.

Times up,

As the fetish of a haughty universe,

speculating with four fins and a tail.

Had 'four eyes' but was still blind,

learned to be prey without a prayer of a choice,

until I could stand on two hind legs.

Took a deep breath, chest puffed up,

pouted my lips and walked beyond the ocean shore.

Took another Kali Yuga plus 26,000 years,

to finally speak and all I could say is,

"Survival of the fittest" and

"Every man for himself,"

a rehash of past lives and transgressions,

Natural Selection without introspection.

Seems like we've not evolved whatsoever.

Description

Evilution explores the seeming non-progression of humanity's empathy, selfish and violent tendencies and behaviours despite evolving biologically, physically and even intellectually. Demonstrating the futility and supercell nature of so-called "progress."

Déjà vu

Haven't I seen you before?

Perhaps or perchance, we had crossed paths when I caught your
scent?

Unearthly, pharaonic, and Lovecraftian,

And seeping through the pores of your skin.

Sweet and sticky, like molten brown sugar,

Yet sharp like whiskey and moonshine.

As your shadow lanced across its bright and blushing face,

Turning crescents into smiles

As you smile and turn to your left and to your right,

Port and starboard,

Eyes sailing towards the Eastern stars that pierced a smoggy
London sky.

She was an Aquarius, in name, in form, and in age.

And she was arched over, suggestively posed.

And poised, delicately, amongst the cloth of the night.

Wrapped up like dark matter and "Blue Steel" in a Playboy centrefold.

She'd waited 2,160 years to return to her first love.

Only to be rejected by another.

One whose words flowed like rivers.

And we had been happy to sup on her waters.

As both fish and men, and then as fishes of men.

But just as waters break, so too does new life create new thirst.

It's just that we don't thirst for change.

So, she went her own way, dissolving back into the thick black firmament.

Leaving behind a fierce gale, punctuated by sharp, white hot, and forking tongues.

That spoke of harsh truths in strange riddles and memes.

A seeming recompense for us who were,

Unprepared for her earnest return.

Description

Déjà Vu aligns love at first sight with love of self, or love of the divine, or a 'truth.' It signifies love being ready for us (love, truth or enlightenment), but us not being ready for love. In this sense, at this time and in this age, we both become "star-crossed."

Niki Chesworth aka The Ode Biddie

Introduction

NIKI CHESWORTH aka The Ode Biddie

As a young girl it was the Romantics – Wordsworth, Coleridge, Byron, Keats – then in my teens the Liverpool Poets – particularly Roger McGough who I saw in a pub as a teen (I still have the book I bought for just £1.95) – and then, studying A Levels, the war poets particularly Wilfred Owen. So, poetry, in all its infinite variety, has always been a part of my life.

But it was only when Jackie Lowe asked if I would write a poem for the first event that she staged at The Bedford – and perform it to a live audience, that I realised this is what I want to do: write spoken word poetry. I'd never stood up in front of an audience and read my own words before, but my musings about the realities of life in my sixties somehow turned out to be funny and became a regular feature of The Creative Souls events.

Down with The Kids (Not)

OK, I might be a bit delulu, but I believe I can be boujee

See, I know street vernacular even though I'm over sixty

I am now so woke, I get down with Gen Alpha and Zee

I think I'm gas, dank, the CEO of the hood's vocabulary

So, I ask my boys 'What slang would describe your ma?'

I was hoping they'd say I had rizz – as in charisma

But they just moaned about my attempts to be trendy

And said 'The new word for people like you is CHEUGY'

What? I secretly Googled to find out what it means

Apparently, it's for us oldies still wearing skinny jeans

Who have 'live, laugh, love' signs and sport slogan tees

CHEUGYs are outdated, basic, trying too hard to please

That's when I realised, I'm not slaying it with my 'fam'

Suppose I should be grateful they didn't call me Karen

And accept that words mean different things today

Admit that I want to ask, 'Sorry, what did you say?'

You see, when I was young, dope was what you smoked

Weed that you rolled into a joint and then toked

But today? Well, dope now means cool… as in sick

No, I don't mean puking up or anything like 'The Ick'

Instead, today dope means lit, rad, banging or stellar

Yeah, it's confusing innit, this Gen Alpha vernacular?

Me, I still think salty describes crisps and the like

But today, apparently, it means jealous or up for a fight

And in my youth, drips were a complete waste of space

But now dripping shows you shop in the right place

While I thought busing, it was jumping on the 49

Today, it means you're the GOAT or the greatest of all time

As a kid, a snack was a nibble before you were fed

Today, it's slang for an attractive person you want to bed

But on the positive side, thicc no longer means dumb

Instead, it's a compliment for us with curves and a bum

And I remember my mum calling me a spoilt brat

But it's been redefined as confident, hedonistic …I'll take that

Yet, it's not easy for us oldies to understand this lingo

We may dress like teens and are too young for bingo

But we hear 'hip' and think of the orthopaedic department

And for us, pads are for incontinence – and not an apartment

No wonder they want to cancel us, our vibe is all wrong

We are past it - a bit MEH – particularly if we still wear a thong

But I'm not gonna change even though they might dis me

And I'm happy they've invented a word for just me, CHEUGY

So watch out, kids: I'm a salty, thicc, wannabe brat who's no snack

Bussing it with my free bus pass, something you Gen Alpha's lack.

Fright Night

On Halloween night, I wake with a start

A dry mouth and a pounding heart

There's something prowling in my house

And from the growling, it isn't a mouse

A deep grrr grrr grrr sound

A rumbling that's shaking the ground

Terrified, shivering, I sit bolt upright

Gingerly lean over, turn on the light

I hold my breath, expecting violence

But instead…there is only silence

I listen… no, there's nothing there

Creep out of my room, look down the stairs

Still nothing! So, I sit and await my fate

Upright in bed, determined to stay awake

I'm tense, alert, but eventually start to doze

My head rests on the pillow, and my eyes close

Then, I hear grrr grrr grrr close to my head

My god, whatever it is, it's right here in my bed

I scream, jump out, and yank the covers away

Maybe it's just a fox, a cat or a stray

Waiting for a sudden flash of fur, I stare

But once again… there is nothing there

I'm beginning to think it's my imagination

That I've conjured up a ghostly apparition

Telling myself to stop being so daft and silly

I lie back down, try to sleep, but inevitably

The grrr grrr grrr starts once again

I try to work out what it is.. and then…

I realise it's not a monster, a ghost or a goul

What an idiot I am …I'm a total fool

That rumbling sound like a beast's deep roar

It's coming from me… Oh my God… I've started to snore!

Description

I process what it's like being a sexagenarian (that's a woman in her 60s… so no sex is involved!) through humour – one poem explores the way language differs across the generations (and how out of touch that makes you feel) and how ageing often affects you in surprising ways.

Oliver Tuffen

Introduction

Oliver Tuffen is a Surrey-based monochromatic mixed media artist who crafts compelling visual narratives. His work tells stories through images, drawing from personal experiences and observations. Oliver seeks subjects with stories etched in their eyes and facial features, or, when working with objects, he focuses on textures and shapes that inherently tell a story.

His pieces capture profound depth and emotion, inviting viewers to connect with the narratives embedded within each creation. This unique approach has garnered international recognition, with exhibitions in galleries from London to Paris and Tokyo.

Oliver is the youngest gallery-represented artist to be signed to a globally known agency, solidifying his status as a remarkable emerging talent in the art world.

Patricia Ahern

Introduction

Patricia Ahern, Mental Fitness Coach, published author, and podcaster, describes herself as a creative thinker who turns her creative thoughts into creative writings in the form of poetic stories. Her poetic stories are based on true life experiences, filled with passion for forward-focused thinking and action. They are written with food for thought to inspire a positive mindset with compassion, empowerment, growth, development and self-love. When Patricia cultivated self-love within, she found her passion and purpose in life and uses her gift and talent now as a creative writer and mental fitness coach to inspire others to do the same. Tune in to her Mindful Poetic Stories Podcast on this link: https://mindfulpoeticstoriespodcast.podbean.com/ and available on all Podcast Platforms.

Apple, Spotify, Amazon Prime, etc., or check out my website
https://www.pacoaching.co.uk/

Through Your Paintings

I see you, I hear you, I feel you,
but I do wonder can I ever truly understand.
So I try to put myself in your shoes
and wonder, imagine, what that must be like

to lose everything you own, life shattered,

have everything you love taken away from you

along with your home.
But then a thought,

maybe you don't want me to put myself in your shoes

but instead to awaken to such brutal atrocities,

people torn between countries
in battle, borne out of war and greed

by the – *"powers that be"* monstrosities.
Wishing, wanting, craving, to go home

even if it is to the nothingness.
But yet at the same time,

driven by the instinctual need to survive,

to build a new life somewhere alien.
Start over, despite those feelings of nothingness

but with the strength of your physical body,

the skin on your bones and the clothes on your back
you still have that, despite what else you lack.
I know what it is like to be torn between people in battle

fighting for what they believe is right, what they believe is true
and the anger and devastation this can fuel

one coming from the east - the other from the west
seeing things the complete opposite, never meeting in the middle
but hating each other with such zest
both fighting to have their say
the absolute power to have things their own way,
never considering the human desire,

to live - in love - in peace.
So yes, I see you, I hear you, I feel your desire

to creatively express yourself
so that all humanity can hear you, feel you, see you
and know that in this world
- there is hate and there is love
- there is evil and there is love
- there is hurt and there is love
- there is pain and there is love
- there is an enemy and there is an ally
to our human experience, all of these will forever apply
these are what we will see time and time again
until the love of imagination, curiosity, creativity reign
in our minds, hearts and souls, a constant, ever to remain
so that people can feel it, they can see it, they can hear it,
and know it's energetic positive power
– for human connection.
So yes, through your paintings I see you and I see hope
that all this dawns on humanity and we all awaken to its beauty
hope's energy.
It's power to build, not break the spirit of community
it's power to ever and always create.

In times of great divides and destructions by evil forces
creativity does help us to create something better
to know and share and feel nothing but hope.

And even though some paintings on me heavy weigh
I feel what you are hoping to portray.

We here with our things and our things and our more things
Do we remember there are people without things, without excess
things,
living without consumerism!
So they ask,

What is poison? The excess of anything you actually need.
What is scarcity? Less than what you need.
What is war? Your basic needs taken away from you

These things make it difficult to survive
and so you sure as hell can't thrive.

Here today miles apart - I support you
from my creative soul and heart
I send you love through the whispers of the frequency,

vibrancy, energy of this beautiful magical universe,

from my atoms to your atoms, in this moment

we are connected, even though I may not see your face
but by the power of creative transference, and grace,
know I see you, I hear you, and for the love of humanity,

I love you and support your work
I love your determination to survive despite life's evil forces
and to live without excess things, but only for your love of life.
That's too what I want to live for, *Love*.
Yours creatively

Written 02.03.25

Inspired by Kakuma Art Project – Art-A-Thon Fundraiser

<u>***Description***</u>

In May 2023, I met Tara Dominick, an artist who had set up the Kakuma Art Project in collaboration with Generation Aid, raising money to run therapeutic art workshops for creatives in the Kakuma Refugee Camp in Kenya. I was so inspired by Tara's work and passion, I bought her painting called the "Boat," which she was selling to raise money. This "Boat- The Power of One Painting" fundraising project was so successful that Tara decided to continue the fundraising by organising an Art-A-Thon in March 2025, where creators/artists around the UK took part in a 10-hour marathon of creating in all different genres. I, myself, did ten hours of creative writing, which I thoroughly enjoyed, and on 1st March 2025, I could feel the positive energy of all those creating.

One of the writing project challenges I had set myself on the day was an "ekphrasis," which refers to a literary device where a work of art is described in a literary text. On looking through the paintings which had already transpired from the Kakuma Art Project workshops, I just couldn't choose one, as they all inspired me so much, and therefore what was created from looking through all the paintings from the first Kakuma Art Workshop was this poetic story, which I titled, "Through Your Paintings." You can find out more about Tara and the Kakuma Art Project on this link: https://www.taradominickartist.com/projects

And you can hear me recite Through Your Paintings on this link:

https://kakumaartproject.com/performance-poetry/

Ode to the Greats

Oh, the greats, the greats

With their legacies and fates

Their stories, their movements

their humanitarian improvements

so captivating, inspiring, rewiring,

live on in our history books and beyond

I remember their souls with my heart so fond.

I have a dream - the most memorable

demonstration of emancipation ever seen

Lincoln, who cast that first beacon of light and hope

so slaves no longer had to grope,

for freedom, basic human rights

Even the right to live....

in equality with, holier than thou, supremacy.

Mandela, who took his long walk to freedom

leaving bitterness behind in the very jail of his jailors.

He said, 'May your choices reflect your hopes, not your fears.'

I say, may the love of your heart bring peace, not anguished tears

May humanity grow, and hate dissolve in the coming years.

When we stop feeding negativity with negativity

And we stop feeding hate with hate,

And fear with fear….

It is then, and only then, that it has a chance to stop growing

love will have a beautifully lit space to keep flowing

As we cannot drive out the darkness with the dark

Only our light can do that…

So what are we to do?

Well, I say, find that light inside you, and **Let It Shine** ….

Emmeline Pankhurst said, Remember the dignity of womanhood,

do not appeal, do not beg, do not grovel, take courage, join hands.

Yes, let's join forces…

Millicent Fawcett said, Courage calls to courage everywhere, and
its voice cannot be denied.

Let these heartfelt courageous words, your heartful spirit, and your
mind guide.

Mother Teresa said, - Peace starts with a smile.

Are we fearing the future because we are wasting our today?

We fear and hate so deep, due to our inner unhealed pain

our masked wounds of distress & trauma, that's what I say… **here today**

as having lived in fear my whole life - I now ask myself;

Do I wish to live in fear - or - die in love – in hope?

Emancipate yourself from inner slavery; none but ourselves can free our minds

Oh, the greats, the greats, and their fates

they laid down paths, so much sacrificed, for **our freedom**

But yet we live on, still so weighed down by hate

but is it time to ask yourself, what do you want for your fate

Cause, we too can be great…………. for the next generation

We too can **speak up and speak out** with words, in a love demonstration

Like Martin Luther's in 1963 to a nation

What will be your personal nisus?

You know, the two Chinese symbols for crisis are;

danger and opportunity

I say, in times of crisis may humans take the opportunity

to build, not break, the love within, the spirit of community

may we all too decide to leave a legacy of **love's unity**

As Maya Angelou said, Love recognises no barriers.

It jumps hurdles, leaps fences, and penetrates walls to arrive at its
destination full of hope

We know the destination, this life will come to an end

I say, let's decide now, our legacy

For me, moving from egotism to altruism,

Yes, **I do too have a dream–**

Do you?

12.12.23
<u>*Description*</u>

All my life, I have been drawn towards inspirational quotes. I
didn't realise how far back this went until my wonderful discovery
in my mum's house of some old diaries written by my 14-year-old
self. I found within the pages of these old diaries inspirational
quotes that I had cut out of magazines. I would have never
remembered I did this at such a young age, but the evidence was
there, and in itself, inspiring.

Since I started writing in 2021, I toyed with the idea of writing a
poetic story with inspirational quotes weaved in but it wasn't until

December 2023 when I was invited to a local poetry open mic with the theme of Justice – the flyer said Black Christmas - "The arc of the moral universe is long but it bends towards justice" Martin Luthor King. Instantly, I was inspired, and Ode to the Greats was born; it pretty much wrote itself from that inspirational moment.

It is my ode and salute to the people of history who stood up for what they believed in; they moved the way love makes us move, not how fear makes us move. These people paved the way for us.

The people whose words of wisdom still live on and have the ability to inspire us long after they have passed. Those words help to change the trajectory of the lives of generations after them for the better.

I wish to be part of that movement, living from love, wisdom and inspiration, starting with self-love. We all get a cup in life; it's our responsibility to fill it with what we want more of. As what you have in your cup will be what is poured out.

I believe how we fill our cup is what legacies are made of.

Peter Burns

Introduction

I am a recently retired teacher trying to write poems that have rhythm, rhyme and relatability – in the hope that readers and listeners may find some humour, some passion, some resonances and possibly some new perspectives.

Lyle

Every once, folks, every once in a while

comes an imagination, so fertile

whose musical soul cannot but beguile.

A voice, a mind, that's just so versatile.

So let's settle down and listen awhile

cos I tell you, it will be, worth your while—

Let's all give thanks to our beautiful Lyle

From that first San Lorenzo's, delicate fascination,

borne to the jazz world, from its midwestern derivation.

With its floating, dreamlike, glistening air.

A new jazz vocabulary, a psalm, a prayer.

A fresh and original gift out of nowhere,

from the first jazzer I'd seen, with a rocker's long hair

A painter of sonic pictures, a writer of euphoric stories

that resonate and inspire, as both past and present glories.

A composer, performer, fellow-musician-enthuser

A multiple-faceted, keyboard cruiser

A pool player, soccer player, Lego fan.

Architect, computer whizz, Renaissance man.

A mind and soul, and body... that was able to invent

The structure and emotion evoked by a creation like 'Ascent'!

So, whatever you're up to, Lyle, way up there,

we will all continue this sweet love affair

with your poignant pieces, too many to mention

that take our spirit through an extra dimension

As we relish, and savour and continue to extol

your delicacy of musical mind - musical soul

saved for special moments, just like… a profiterole!

As you sit content on your piano stool, at the concert's end, the
concert's ovation

A picture of natural, unforced cool, with your double-thumb-
rolling appreciation

So, just let me think, let me relish, 'Let Me Count The Ways'

that our lives have been enhanced by the music of Lyle Mays

Thank you, Lyle

https://www.youtube.com/watch?v=xALBQkpi68M

Description

'Lyle' is a celebratory eulogy to the late Lyle Mays who, as a founding
member of the Pat Metheny Group, was a multiple Grammy winning
composer, arranger and performer of mould breaking 'jazz-fusion' pieces
that had a kind of magical sweet spot involving Midwestern sincerity and
Classical principles.

I saw him many times live and still listen to much of his music.

The Fluke

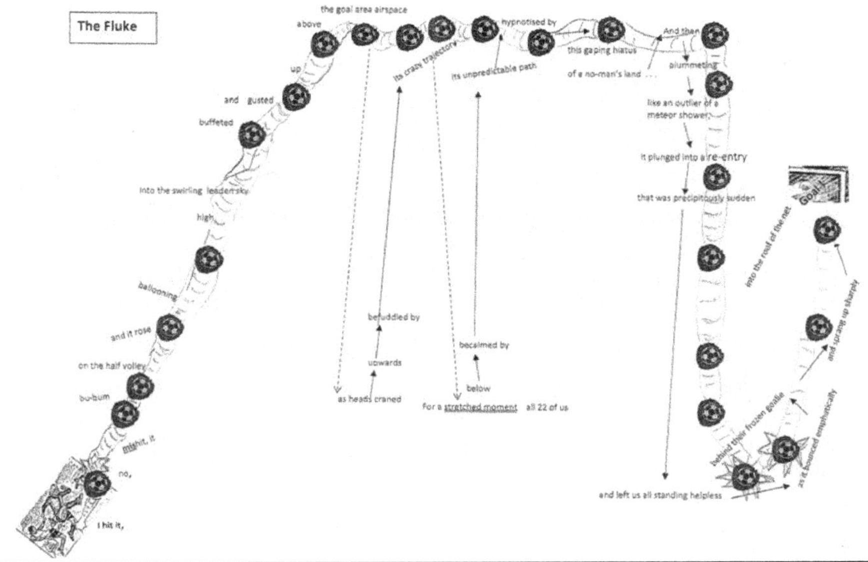

Description

‘**The Fluke**’ was the winning goal I scored in the under 15, Whitehaven Schools District Final, in extra time—and, as you will see, when you read the visual and lyrical trajectory of the ball, it was a real Fluke!

Romano Giorgi

Introduction

Romano Giorgi is a Balham-based self-help author, podcaster and singer/songwriter. His book and podcast are both titled 'The Much Better You - your wellbeing and mental health sorted.' His book is available from Waterstones, Clapham Books and Amazon. And you can check out his podcast, rock band 'LEIKA' and solo music projects 'Romano Is Solo' on all the well-known digital music platforms, plus LEIKA often play shows in London.

The Rarest Loop

Somewhere between stations,
my body rests in metal silence—
yet my mind drifts
into a world
I do not know,
and somehow always have.

I sit beside strangers
who smile with a history
my waking self never lived.
Their names rise like smoke,
vivid for a breath,
then vanish.
But in that world,
we've shared decades.
We've argued,
laughed,
grown old together
in seconds.

And then—
the brakes hiss.
A jolt.
The train opens its mouth
to the grey platform,
and I awaken,
hollowed out by absence.

They were real.
Weren't they?

What was that place
where my whole being lived
just moments ago?
A parallel plane
folded softly inside my skull,
a life pressed between pages
I never meant to open.

Is this the dream?
Am I the flicker
in someone else's wandering mind—
a shadow self
who thinks himself the main act
while another me wakes
from this?

And sometimes—
without sleep,
without warning—
the veil thins again.

I'll be somewhere ordinary—
in a meeting,
or walking through trees—
then suddenly,
a bloom of seeing.
The room no longer just a room,
but a stage
set with miracles:
hands that move,
lips that form thought,
light that rests on a cheek.

And I am in it,
but also watching it—
aware of being aware:
the rarest loop.

And in those moments,
the world is impossibly beautiful
and impossibly strange.

And I wonder
if we're nothing more
than passing shadows
in each other's dreams—
lives flickering against the dark,
touched by love for a moment,
then lost again
to the silence we came from.

Description

The first poem, **The Rarest Loop,** reflects on some thoughts
Romano had about how sometimes our daydreams seem to capture,
then near instantly dismiss an entire lifetime of memories in but a
single moment, and how sometimes we may find ourselves
observing ourselves and others objectively it seems.

EasyJet

As EasyJet's wings dip low to land,

My sunlit days, once carefully planned,

Now vanish behind, like mist on the sea,

Much like my tan — it won't last, set it free.

"Fasten your belts!" the captain's command,

But spot the twat— with brains he's not armed.

Phone in his palm, no flight mode to find,

Excuse me, sir! Are you out of your mind?

The plane hits the tarmac, applause fills the air,

Bags jostle loose, but stay in your chair.

Twat man is poised, the Exit he clocks

Like Linford Christie, twitching at his blocks.

The seatbelt sign dims, and he's up in a flash,

Compartment pops open, he makes a mad dash.

His briefcase drops, a direct hit to the head,

Down he goes, all arse and dread.

Arse over tit, tit over arse,

He sprawls in the aisle — no one may pass.

With poise and grace, an attendant pulls him near,

Returns him to his seat, but he offers no cheer.

I step to the ramp, Heathrow air crisp and bright,

An attendant leans in, keeping whispers light:

"Best call a medic; he's taken a knock."

"Seat 12A?" I ask. "Yeah… that's the cock."

Sean Byrne

Don't Come Copper on a Copper

Passed out at Hendon when I was 19

Shiny new truncheon and a fistful of dreams

Bang up the villains and keep the streets clean

Like Dirty Harry and Steve McQueen

Luther and Dixon, Lewis and Morse

Must be some way to get on in the force proceeding left, I'm a
westerly direction

Getting dogs abuse and little affection

Plodding the heat, soaking wet

Sod this mate, I'm off to the Met

Took the exams and passed the lot

Bright new future. I'll give it a shot

Decent send-off. Everyone pissed

Word in your ear. Was there something I missed?

Old Sergeant said as I cleaned out my locker

Don't come Copper on a Copper

Along the mean streets, down in the ditches,

Built up my contacts, ran my snitches

Saved my arse by the seat of my britches

Fast track promo, back the right horse

Work all hours. No time for skivers

Pushing the envelope full of unmarked fivers

Dig and delve, duck and dive with AC12 and M15

Divvy out the takings in a smoky dive

Scale the ladder, rung by rung

OCG always there with a bung

Tell me a porky, I'll tell you a whopper

But don't come Copper on a Copper

Jump the rope, duck thru the hoops

Stop right there. Don't move or I'll shoot

Go underground, infiltrate some feminist groups

Brand new mane of hair, spreading my seed who knows where

Demos and meetings, skirts and blouses

Hard to keep it in my trousers.

Up the duff, down the chute

Not me guv, I'm out of the loop

Out of my depth, it's getting too hard

Gotta get your arse back to the yard

Didn't even leave a calling card

You may say I was a bit of a rotter

But I didn't come Copper on a Copper

Get down the clubs and sort out the fights

Have a quick word and shoot out the lights

All night stake outs, fags and booze

Marriage sliding gently down the tubes

She thought I was a flipper but she found was a flopper

But she didn't come Copper on a Copper

Such thrills and spills, banter and fun

But a copper's lot is not a happy one

I've run out of lives, dobbed in by my mates

Left ne hanging by the prison gates

Banged up in the Scrubs, still slopping out

This must be what it's all about

Looks like I messed up good and proper

And someone came Copper on a Copper.

We Need to Talk About Starmzy

Looks good in a suit, a suitable contender

Should win the election, let's see his agenda

No windfall tax, no taxes on wealth

How we gonna pay for the National Health?

Reverse all those cuts in overseas aid?

We're not quite ready for that, I'm afraid.

Water companies dump shit in our rivers

I know we should nationalise, but it gives me the shivers

Don't "frighten the horses," or else we'll be toast

Same with the energy, the trains and the post

Broken Britain not easy to fix it

And please don't say a word about Brexit

Das ist nicht gut, versteihen sie?

We really need to talk about Starmzy

Got to balance the budget and look respectable

We'll be making changes, but they won't be perceptible.

Schools are crumbling, housing in chaos

Fat cats squat on the land awaiting payoffs

But there's no need to get into a spasm

Word of the day is curb your enthusiasm

It's enough to send you on a raid to the pharmacy

We need to have a word about Starmzy.

Rowing back on the climate when you could be a hero

Nah! We'll take the slow lane to net zero

Steady as she goes, can't go on a bender

Never learnt the words to Hey Big Spender

Some want him soaked in a butt of Malmsey

That's from Shakespeare, you may know it slightly

Or just me wearing my learning lightly

Still all these statements add to my mirth

Our demands are moderate, we only want the Earth

Yes! It's time to have a word with Starmzy

Sila Guiance

Introduction

Sila is a Life Success Coach at designthebestyou.com, working with ambitious individuals who want to create extraordinary lives.

After a long and successful career in the civil service and subsequently as a property investor, **Sila** turned her focus to her lifelong passion: helping others transform their lives from the inside out. Drawing on rich personal experience, professional reinvention, and extensive training, she
founded DesignTheBestYou.com—where she empowers individuals to uncover their true calling and achieve meaningful life goals.
Her work is rooted in growth, clarity, and living with intention.

You can connect with Sila on
LinkedIn www.linkedin.com/in/silaguiance or get in touch for a no-obligation coaching session at info@designthebestyou.com

This Time It's for Real
<u>*Phase 1*</u>

It's a brand-new year, and for all its promise let's all cheer:

Design your own future, it's all in your hands

Your life's a canvas, awaiting your plans.

(And this time it's for real)

It's a brand-new year, a fresh new slate,

A chance to rebuild, to create my own fate.

My goals are clear, my vision is bright,

This time I'll soar; I WILL take the flight.

(And this time it's for real)

It's a brand-new year, this one is the one

A chance to rebuild, the race has begun

I'll rise with the sun, chase every dream,

With boundless drive and a steady stream.

(And this time it's for real)

So it's new new new, new year, new place, new me

It's try, try, try, try diet, try riches, try and see

It's more more more, more dreams, more fame, more free

Phase 2

I'm surely improving. I'm trying so hard. The effort is worth it,
I'm on the right path.

But I have this big problem - haven't got the time

One glass won't count: "It's only this once"

We are humans after all, and it's human to fall.

(But this time it's for real)

I deserve all I want, now and forever more. My dream's just
waiting, I'll give it my all.

What if I quit? Would it matter at all?

What if I stumble, what if I fall?

No one cares, and the effort seems vast,

Fear whispers softly, "You've failed in the past."

(But this time it's for real)

Way too soon, the dream is over. Back on the tube and back on my
rota,

And the days grow heavy, and the pace feels slow,

The fire is dimming, and the doubts start to show.

"Why is it so hard?" my weary heart sighs,

The mirror reflecting all of my whys.

(But this time it's for real)

So it's lack lack lack, lack of time, lack of funds, lack of spark

It's doubt doubt doubt, doubt effort, doubt the journey, doubt the
mark

It's blame blame blame, blame pressure, blame struggle, blame the dark

<u>It wasn't for real</u>

Phase 3

The typical lifecycle of an unfulfilled dream

The higher the hope the deeper the pain

As obstacles show, motivation goes

The path disappears where nobody knows.

"It was not meant to be," evidence of results that couldn't have been.

But why did I start? What truth did I see?
What kind of future'd be waiting for me?

What's holding me back—what do I fear?
What if the answers are already here?
If the path is tough, does it mean I'm lost,
or is it just a challenge worth the cost?

"It wasn't for real, but there's always next year"

No, there isn't. This is it. It's only this moment, and that's all there is.

The weight of regret will grow with the years,

A life unfulfilled by the "if only" tears.

Or just weather the doubt, dance in the rain

Stay your course and push through the pain.

Your future "you" with pride in your chest

Knowing you gave it your absolute best.

No more lack - only light

No more try - only trust

No more doubt - only do

No more new - you will do

And this time it's for real.

Dreams

"Sweet dreams are made of this"

They're the key in life to succeed:

It's easier than you may have thought

This simple: what do you want?

It's not a house, not a car, not a holiday,

or it may be, but why?

Why, why, why — why many times

to get to the root of what your you truly minds.

Do you dream enough? Or even not at all?

Do you listen to your dream? Do you sit with it, or just let it go?

Do you give it airtime, so it can show you your life?

Because dreams reveal the truth inside

The life you're meant to live

They're for a reason in your mind.

They're the results you're meant to achieve.

But way too often we don't stop, and instead we run in place.

After the pre-designed life, that easily comes our way.

Our dreams are deeper than we think

They tell us what we need to see

They show us the light to follow

Our desires are deeper than we think; it's the universe talking to us,

You'll need to dig deep within and simply listen to your you.

If you're willing to go after it, you're on your own journey

But if you don't - it will die inside of you.

Simone Graham

Introduction

Poetry comes to me in moments I can't predict—words flowing through the heart, not the mind, landing on paper like they've been waiting to speak. As a woman of the hospitality world, I've spent years connecting with people from all walks of life. Those shared stories and fleeting moments awakened my deep love for perspective and the power of human experience.

I write to explore how we see, feel, and exist in the world— trusting the spark of inspiration when it arrives, while also nurturing my creative voice with presence and practice.

Breathe

I'm suffocating,

Eyes dilating,

The pressure climbs

No sense of time,

No pulse,

No signs.

I'm fading.

Can't seem to breathe,

A whisper crawls inside my ear,

A lump that swells within my throat

The words dissolve, replaced by fear.

And in the distance,

Hope, unclear.

A whisper in my hollow chest,

A tremble where my soul once slept,

A power sparked I can't suppress

One I buried,

One I kept.

Still suffocating,

Heart palpitating.

Frozen still…

Silent will.

A vision… me,

Just lying there,

Lifeless, weightless,

Stripped and bare.

Then

Something.

A breath of air,

It weaves through wounds I tried to hide,

Reviving pieces left to die,

A resurrection deep inside.

A surge I fail to comprehend,

Yet somehow, now, I ascend.

A gasp of life floods through my chest,

Each inhale guiding me to rest.

The veil of pain begins to cease,

And with each breath,

I welcome peace.

Enlightened.

Empowered.

Energy freed.

I once was drowning in the dark…

But because of you,

I now

Breathe.

Description

This poem is a descent and a rising, a journey through suffocation, silence, and the fragile line between breaking and becoming. "Breathe" was born in a moment where words felt too heavy to speak, yet too urgent to stay buried. As someone who moves through the world constantly connecting with others, I've learned that even in spaces full of people, we can feel isolated, unheard, unseen.

This piece captures what it feels like to lose your voice, your grounding, your self, and then, slowly, to reclaim it. It's about the invisible battles, the quiet whispers of strength, and the breath that carries us back to life when we least expect it.

Bath Time

Generational disaster

Chasing after the one

I laugh

We bathe in the heat

Of excitement

Delighted

A new fresh scent

We bend

Our boundaries

Trapped in the bubbles

We float

Unaware of the internal drowning

Of our inner self

The temperature too hot for our liking

But we pretend, smiling

Accepting this is it

Trying to scrub away

What we once were

To accommodate another

A lover

A robber

Free to step out

Not his

But mine

We dry

Oh we try

But still damp

The scent like a stamp

Smelling fresh

But a reminder of the death

Of whom we were

Looking back

At what was once clear water

Now dirty

Too deep to see

Dead cells now gone

Walking away lighter

Somewhat brighter

Covered in your scent

Till the very end

Description

"Bath Time" dives into the illusion of intimacy, the way we lose parts of ourselves trying to fit into someone else's idea of love. It's about the quiet unravelling that happens when we pretend comfort in something too hot, too heavy.

This poem reflects the tension between connection and self-abandonment, and the strength it takes to step out, still damp, still marked, but finally your own.

Tanvir Akram

Introduction

Tanvir is from Derby and started writing after a battle with cancer almost took his voice.

He started posting online, under the moniker 'Silent One' in 2015.

He now runs two spoken word nights to encourage people to speak their 'truth.'

He aspires to bring people together from different backgrounds to create tolerance and understanding.

Lullaby of Waves

An echo of footsteps fill the serene, salty air,

muffled thuds like faint taps in slow motion,

moving in a sombre sonata over a creaking pier. The bitter breeze
is a harbinger of forthcoming storms,

but in an empty promenade, the silence is soothing.

My anchor heart finds comfort at the sun shimmering,

upon a lullaby of waves calming the senses,

I lose my thoughts, almost forget myself,

as they softly caress moist sands,

sinking deep into trodden grains,

each ripple touching my hollow soul

like messengers of prophecies,

with sweet premonitions of pleasure and treasure,

but some resemble embers eternally burning,

leaving behind a directory of debris,

engraving intensely, as each fragment

weighs me down like burdens from a wreckage.

The mind ponders,

how I am a northern shore

whilst my life is a southern coastline.

What could have been and what will be,

what is mine and what is not,

what I actually deserve and what I have got.

In these internal fragilities,

we are like estuaries without an embankment.

But in this stillness, the sunset is evidence

how the end can be graceful.

I gaze towards the ceaseless seas,

wishing the tide could carry me away,

but I am a broken boat left to rot

upon cold sands on a winter's day.

<u>*Description*</u>

I went on a road trip to the northeast, and one morning, I decided to go to Saltburn beach. As I walked along the pier, it was a cold morning, but the sun was shining bright. I looked out at the sea, pondered about life and where I am, and where I would like to be. The poem is about wanting to be in a good place but not knowing how you will escape your current dilemma. I used my inner voice to mirror the natural surroundings around me.

Ivory Flakes

In the mirrors of Moirai

kismet and karma kiss adoringly,

unaware of this betrayal they label as life.

In the hallucination we call birth,

words whisper like bitter winds,

composing a metaphorical manuscript,

weaving a quilt of invisible inflictions.

Silent screams serenade in childhood bloodshed,

where no messiah arrived to rectify sins of saints –

so some languish among abandoned souls.

Modern monsters no longer hide beneath the bed,

they feast amongst our freshly prepared banquets.

In a fathomless pit, I'm slaying prosaic demons,

before indigo hues turn ebony –

who are they to destroy my dreams?

I never heard the birds sing

in a playground of lucid lullabies.

I still recall the ghosts of featherless angels,

swaying upon swings adorned in garlands of grief.

Their eternal spirits flickering in silver embers,

evolving into perpetual vessels of reflection.

Confused in a realm of revolving doors,

tarnished paths only withhold wrath,

leaving behind trails of trauma,

where twisted trials lead to disfigured destinies.

Glass hearts only break in battles with burdens,

so our spirits become victim to Medusa eyes.

When each sigh flows like a slow poison,

we search for virgin daffodil dawns,

as distractions to numb the pain.

Fatigued from the battles from

those who rebel against our hearts –

we seek solace from sojourners of invigoration.

Blessed are those who connect with universal harp strings.

Who merge with the sacred aura of music.

Who notice the stars before twilight,

comprehending the glory of sunrise,

as an analogy against adversity.

I was not designed to be a flower,

contained in a snow globe,

covered in ivory flakes when shaken.

I have forgiven the blameworthy,

who are guilty for chaining an inner child,

but I'm still waiting to break free.

Before I waste away and my thorns decay,

ordain upon me the fortune to cradle love –

let me flourish in the field where Rumi's roses bloom.
Description

I wrote this poem to give a voice to pain, transformation, and yearning. It's a deeply introspective exploration of suffering, spiritual survival, and the hope for transcendence. Sometimes the ache is too big to carry in silence, so we express what we suppress through poetry.

Tasha Bertram

Introduction

Tasha is a former classical ballet dancer cum actress and
singer/songwriter, and many of her poems are translated and
adapted from her songwriting.
However, she started writing poems from the age of six, when she
fell in love with William Blake. Tasha found that from an early
age, reading poems was far more manageable than getting through
a whole book, and to this day she has incorporated poetry into her
creative life.

Lady Faith

Lady Faith is a Golden Lady
with open arms assured.
The smile she carries in her face
travels in space to mine.
Her roots nestle into the soil of my home.
For today, at least, my life expands, while
pleasure rises, pouring its heat into my void.
Unopened petals part and big soft cushions catch me, as I
let go.
I am
so light. So light I float and know, so know
the wonders of the day and night that
now invite
me in.

What a lovely place you're living.
What sweet smells surround you that hold my trembling hand.
They carry me over the Everglades
to dance on dry land.
Carry me on to where we all belong,
and when I fall, as bound I am,
then sink I shall.
But if I do not feel your reach to pull me out with all your might,
then I might
spring myself into your open arms and
float in your faith once more.

This repetitive pattern of ups and downs and ins and outs and all
arounds, is to

Accept, not to control, the dedication of your soul.
Let it be.
We cannot take the hold of that much power.
That is you.
But you are me, and he is she and us and them, so
let me in
when you hear my call
with the brush of a whisper on your breath.
Or the heat of your disapproval,
that I am not allowed to fall and fall again. Again.
With this I hear you say;

There's no more time for this audacious play.
Stand with poise, share your goods.
Wear your low line vintage dress.

Wipe your tear drop face in upwards strokes,

towards the temple where your smile caresses.
Roll out your carpet into the globe
so that fingers and toes can touch along dusty roads.

I hear you, Lady Faith.
I see your smile throw open gifts I saw wrapped before,
so tightly in a bowline knot.
But with one moment of your grace,
All ties unknot.
Beauty showers explode across the sky,
as Glow Worms fly
Courage to another's field
where in a thousand smiling faces,

tears of pain and healed and
More my doubts revealed.
For Lights go on in many sealed brains,
Washed with lies for the sake of ignorance to remain.
Yes. This, is the damage that melts the buttons on my coat,
which gladly I watch as it falls to the ground
like a bowl of split milk.
The satisfaction on my skin turns bold,
stepping out of this coatless hold.
Towards another day.
When you will hear me say;

I am here to trust in Faith.
Let not my trust be lost in this sad life of rules, that hide the Love-
Light behind a deeper fear of pain.
It's time to change the Shadows who reign.

Ava and the Cyclamen

Thank you for giving me reason to rise,
You and the Cyclamen flower.
Your tiny coloured learned heads,
of pink, white, wild lilac or red,
Wait for nothing.
Deep in vibrancy, bright with reason,
You hold yourselves through every month
against the weather of each season.
When all else hang their pretty heads and shiver,
Your upright body is the image of hope,
peeking through the dying stems of another life that cannot cope.

You and you, stand faithful in my dark hour.
Bestow upon me a glimmer for my day.
You hold yourselves tall in your tiniest flame,
as you're seen effortlessly gathered in your crowd again. And yet,
Alone you stand with equal power.
An example of life.
A little flower.

I drink green tea. I wet my cheek
with a single drop that continues to leak.
And this must stop!
When to crawl from my bed
with the ache in my back, my soul and my head,
keeps me
from wanting to find you. And yet,
My dear sweet flower, you grow in me too.
And even in a storm you grow.

When I try to justify my
shallow skin,
I could seek more of you,
and place the power of your life in every corner of my room.
Reliable ones, dependable souls,
that poke your heads through ice and snow
and breathe in all the air around -
whatever is there, and still you grow.
With your heart shaped leaves and your heart on your sleeve,
Infinitely giving out to me,
the joy of life.
I do love thee.

Thank you, for giving me reason to rise.
For brightening my view as I sit and gaze,
at the shape of your colour and the life I have made.
The vision of your dance that moves in my sightline,
gifting your glorious Elan
to my old cloak of shame. And yet,
You lift my hidden spirit out from its shattered frame.

Come. Come gather more in my garden
and let my eyes play
with your upward facing petals,
innately twisting to curl your display.
With modesty you stay in your favourite spot,
under the shade of a tree.
Your kindness reaches me.
And there you watch me
fall in love with life
Because of thee.

Terry Tuffen

15 hundred voices!!

15 hundred voices called till silence overruled them all,

the eerie silence from those now left,

just condensation formed by their breath.

Great loss of life, the papers read that those still missing presumed
are dead,

a tragic end that's so unthinkable, from the ship they said it was
unsinkable.

All the years gone by, and the ship still there; people still go down
to look and stare,

Upon this burial place from life's subtraction is nothing more now
than a fairground attraction.

Trees!

Some cultures they find them sacred,

they go to them and pray,

some will tie a ribbon on,

for a loved one passed away.

Now the folks of Madagascar are quite strong in their belief that
the ancient spirits and those of loved ones,

reside within or just beneath.

Some will carve a heart upon them,

and initial their true love,

some people make a shelter,

and in turn will live high up above.

Some people make a living,

without hesitation

as they get machinery in,

and let them loose to cause such devastation.

Some trees are natural food source,

beneficial to your health,

providing you with oxygen,

no matter of your wealth.

Some say it's where outlaws lived,

to steal from the rich to feed the poor,

they also say it's where the monkeys lived,

but sadly that's no more.

Some trees are decorated,

in the season of good will,

some trees are cut up into logs,

to take off the winter chill.

But here in the good old UK,

a religious stump has sure been hit,

because all we use our trees for is to hang up bags of sh*#.

You're out there with your doggies,

just trying to make them toilet,

then you pick it up within the bag,

then upon the tree to spoil it.

It doesn't look appealing,

just to see them hanging there,

but to those I guess who do it,

well they really do not care.

You've gone to all the effort,

to bag it up not leave alone,

so why not take a little more care,

and take the bloody things back home.

Tunde Balogun

Introduction

T. Balogun is a life coach, poet, mentor & educator with over 30 years' experience working across youth, community & educational sectors. Specialising in empowering young people & marginalised communities, she supports individuals to navigate life transitions & achieve their goals through coaching, mentoring & creative expression. T is the author of the poetry books "Blouse 'n' Skirt, Babe!!!" & "Joy an' Pain, Babe!!!" & was named Coach of the Year at the 2022 Active Wandsworth Awards. With a background in psychology & teaching, she brings empathy, insight & humour to her work, using poetry as a powerful tool for healing, growth & connection.

Lasiren

As a child, she was a gift, but you didn't treat her kindly,

family members jealous of her strength, open-mindedness, beauty
& integrity.

They wanted her to conform,

to their blinkered norms…

Put down, insulted, abused & isolated at times,

just because she refused to follow their crazy rules or tow some
broken line.

Unsafe, she wasn't permitted to be her true self at home,

ridiculed, bullied or beaten, she often felt so alone.

Active, musical, creative & artistic, with a thirst for education,

knew she needed an escape plan, to get out of this negative
situation.

Labelled "the black sheep" she didn't care, 'cos she knew her own
mind,

but felt it wasn't in this life, the unconditional love she sought,
she'd find.

Sometimes, those who are meant to love & protect us, are unable
to do so,

it appears as if they don't care, or maybe it's just you they don't
want to see grow.

In the face of adversity, she'd always been brave,

felt she had to leave or end up too early in an unmarked grave.

That night bruised, beaten & broken inside,

she went down to the sea, dived in, the waves were strong & it was
high tide.

On her way to Davy Jones's Locker (drowning), she felt two hands
pulling her further in,

fighting for her life, she didn't really want to die, a permanent
solution to a temporary problem, but one she felt she couldn't win.

Found herself in an underground palace, couldn't believe what she
was seeing within,

those tales her late Grandma told her were true, 'cos right before
her eyes, there was Lasiren.

Unable to speak, she was amazed by Lasiren's black beauty,

Lasiren used this, to help the young woman see & understand
herself more clearly.

Lasiren said "it's not your time yet, you've still got many
important things to do,

& in my role as the Spirit of Femininity, I'm going to bestow these
gifts on you…

Self-love, self-care, luck & good health,

those who have wronged you, will struggle in life, lose their good looks early & may never achieve any wealth."

This wasn't a dream, 'cos she woke up in the hospital bed the following day,

people asking loads of the wrong questions, but not a word did she say.

She'd reemerged a different person & with this newfound courage, she knew what her next steps would be,

the nurse who worked the day shift, was strangely familiar & looked after her tenderly.

When she was ready, she withdrew all her savings, packed a suitcase, got her passport & took that flight, knowing she needed to be far away,

with the power to bring people together, she found that unconditional love & happiness, & when asked this is what she'd say…

"A beautiful Siren with long black hair, saved me from drowning
one night at sea,

she gave me some special gifts & the message to not worry what
some may say, 'cos you're meant to be a part of the LGBTQ+
community...."

Description

Lasiren is a 'true story' that I travelled to Guadeloupe to uncover,
and there I spoke to a Haitian woman. The poem shows that
mermaids can & do exist in different parts of the world & that they
don't all sit on a rock, have blond hair or harm sailors!

Respect the Waters

I heard it on the radio, a dog was in trouble in the Thames one
winter day,

a man jumped in to save it & nearly drowned as the current carried
them away.

Both had to be rescued by the RNLI crew,

founded in 1824, the Royal National Lifeboat Institution, rushed to
their rescue.

It made me think, without them, what would have become of the
man & the dog **which wasn't his**,

& how come such a vital service has to rely on donations &
volunteers, risking their own lives, surely that's taking the piss!

When that alarm sounds, it means someone's in real danger & by
the crew, everything is dropped,

regardless of the weather or the roughness of the sea, these
volunteers never stop.

Distress calls coming in all year long,

'cos out on the water, things can quickly go very wrong...

"A family cut off by the tide,

a hypothermic sailor, with his boat capsized,

a yacht taking on water,

a person in distress & a mother out swimming, now separated from
her daughter,

a small boat run aground, engine smoking & stormy skies ahead,

kayakers in trouble, a kitesurfer in danger, a solo sailor has tripped
& seriously injured his head,

plus, suddenly getting caught up in that riptide, without the
presence of those lifeguards, the surfer would surely have died."

Just a few examples of the calls for help, coming from somewhere
around our coasts, that could occur on any given day,

lifeboat launched, a rescue mission is soon underway by the RNLI,
the charity that saves lives at sea & on the Thames every night &
day.

There's also lifesaving advice that the water safety teams share & teach,

although there are lifeguards, they're not full-time, & it's vital that people feel safe on the beach.

Remember, these people are volunteers who regularly put their own lives in danger,

on-call 24 hours a day, seven days a week, in order to save the life, of a complete stranger.

<u>*Description*</u>

Respect The Waters is written in tribute to & to highlight the work of the RNLI, especially after hearing that story on the radio.

Virna Teixeira

Introduction

Virna Teixeira is a Brazilian poet/ writer, translator and visual artist. She has had collections of poetry published in South America, Portugal and the UK. Her work has appeared in several magazines and anthologies in Brazil and abroad. More recently, she was included in Temporary Archives: Women of Latin America, published in the UK, and had an anthology of her poems (El Mapa Dolorido del Cuerpo) published by the University of Buenos Aires. Virna runs an indie Latin press, Carnaval Press. She lives in London, where she works as a psychiatrist.

Spinning

The drawing of the carousel returns, as if its

motif is being deconstructed in a fluid way

and what repetition was this that was not understood?

The horses tired, turning, my daughter in the saddle

laughing a lot, her joy in the movement

on a carousel on Brighton pier

my little Amazon daughter announcing the future

rational, rotating her holographic fidget spinner

quickly in her fingers, decoding

in seconds the Rubik's Cube that I never solved

I'm a visual thinker, but I don't know Maths

I follow my intuition, but I now discover other logics

my teenage daughter no longer likes carousels

spinning is repeating, I liked to twirl with my arms

open as a child, I tend to think in circles, I listen

to the same song over and over until I get sick of it

Untitled

face down, the impact

of hot stones and oil

cushions – the painful

map of the body

a spa in Africa

or in Jaipur

ayurvedic, meridians

there is no return

after the nigredo

just the magma of the hours

decomposed – boiling

Jackie Lowe

Introduction

My poetry chronicles a journey that began in the aftermath of heartbreak, broken promises, and the sting of betrayal. Along the way, it became a path of self-discovery—a search for meaning that brought healing through the written word. Through this creative process, I found my own voice and connected with a vibrant community of Creative Souls and friends, whose presence and support I deeply cherish.

My Poem

You left with no goodbye

No words to say why

The woman who gave you her love

Thrown away and left to cry

Her heart torn in two

Her head in a spin

Life has to continue

But how do you begin

The years of love

Of devotion and toil

Quickly forgotten

Your blood wants to boil

Your emotions are high

Your confidence low

With the hurt and the pain

There is nowhere to go

How does someone forget

The person you were

The life that they had

Be so cold and so immature

No explanations given

Even upon request

No answers to anything

Your head is a mess

Everything suddenly changes

Your life ripped apart

Your mind confused

Who was this person you gave your heart

It's hard to describe

What it does to your mind

When nothing makes sense

When you know you are kind

The strength it takes

To get up and be

When you are depleted and drained

When there is nothing left of me

The story continues

The nightmare is real

There is no kindness

I am just a hamster on a rotating wheel

Hung out to dry

By someone else's lies

All I wanted

Was answers to know why

Your clothes hung in our wardrobe

For three years I kept it that way

In case you came back

In case the right words you would say

You packed for the weekend

But simply never came back

The rug was pulled

My world went black

You moved onto a new life

One you say is hell

Maybe one day you'll look back

And realise I did do you well

You've told me I am a fake and a fraud

Someone not to trust

But I am real, I am exactly what I seem

It's you who is dark and now I am left thinking, was it ever love or
just lust

I am broken inside

A shell of who I was

I keep thinking why me

Did you do it just because

I wake everyday confused

It feels so unjust

You've broken my mind

My spirit and my trust

You play one off against another

The game never ends

For any sane person

They too would be driven round the bend

Get everyone in a room

Let's see what they say

All with different stories

No one version the same

Then you tell me I am an angel, beautiful, there is nothing wrong
with me

You want to be with me in part

Then why did you say I am crazy

Why break my heart

So confused I am

And probably forever will be

No answers, no closure

No honesty for me

I'll never know you

I sometimes question do you know you

We all seem to know a different you

Which you is true?

Maybe one day

You never know

Something good will come

And real love to me will flow

The Journey

A journey is the travel to a destination
There can be stops along the way
New sights and smells and experiences to uphold
In spaces unknown, we can breathe in a new day

It is an opening of our mind
Exposure to something new
It is a break from the daily grind
Along one of our dreams we can pursue

It is arriving at a place of beauty.
At a landscape of our dreams,
it is a freedom from the burdens of duty.
It is climbing mountains, dipping into oceans and streams.

A journey has a start and an end.
It has places in the middle too.
It can free us to escape and transcend
On one our mind, body and spirit can renew.

It might not be a physical road trip.
It can be purely mental travel too.
A journey of love, growth and enhancement
Into a person where we feel whole and we feel true.

To travel in our minds with no footsteps taken.
We can learn, and we can achieve.
Our spirit and soul can awaken.
We can be wherever and whoever we believe.

We can sail without needing to row.
We can steer our life with no wheel.
We can blaze a trail or just free flow.
We don't need an automobile.

We don't need to pack for a journey or escape.
We can set off standing still.
We don't need a passport or hard shell case.
We just need to have the will.